ROD DAMON TAKES OFF ON THE BIGGEST CASE OF HIS CAREER.

The Coxeman has never before been faced with a mystery like this—three mysteries, in fact. Three beautiful, deadly agents who can take off into the air—just like that—and leave poor Rod high and dry.

Rod must find out their secret—a secret heretofore known only to the birds and the bees. How can these gorgeous girls fly? And who—or what—is behind these flying fleshpots?

Rod must uncover the answers or a valuable secret could drop into enemy hands. But the idea of girls flying like birds is just too much for the Coxeman. For a while he can't lay a finger on the problem, but then he realizes that

WHATEVER GOES UP . . . *must come down!*

Other Books In This Series By
Troy Conway

THE BERLIN WALL AFFAIR

THE BIG FREAK-OUT

THE BILLION DOLLAR SNATCH

THE WHAM! BAM!
THANK YOU, MA'AM AFFAIR

IT'S GETTING HARDER ALL THE TIME

COME ONE, COME ALL

LAST LICKS

KEEP IT UP, ROD

THE MAN-EATER

THE BEST LAID PLANS

IT'S WHAT'S UP FRONT THAT COUNTS

HAD ANY LATELY?

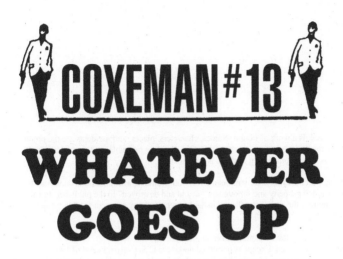

COXEMAN #13

WHATEVER GOES UP

AN ADULT NOVEL BY BY TROY CONWAY

POPULAR LIBRARY

Copyright © 1969 by Coronet Communication, Inc.

Popular Library
Hachette Book Group USA
237 Park Avenue
New York, NY 10017

Popular Library is an imprint of Grand Central Publishing. The Popular Library name and logo is a trademark of Hachette Book Group USA, Inc. The Coxeman name and logo is a trademark of Hachette Book Group USA, Inc.

Visit our Web site at www.HachetteBookGroupUSA.com

First Paperback Printing: June, 1969

Printed in the United States of America

Conway, Troy
Whatever Goes Up/ Troy Conway
(Coxeman, #13)

ISBN 0-446-54317-9 / 978-0-446-54317-0

CHAPTER ONE

I was fishing for a girl.

I was cold, wet, hungry and tired.

I had been on watch here on this Carolina beach the whole night long, and for a long part of this dull, gray morning. I was disgusted with myself, with my assignment, and with the fact that I had to fish without bait.

Maybe I could have hooked onto a bluefish if I had been allowed to use anything more than an empty hook held down by a lead sinker as I reeled it in along the rocky shale in the rough waters off this Outer Bank beach.

Gray driftwood, a leaden sky, the cold white sands of the seashore, were enough to dampen my enthusiasm for my job. I was the only person alive in a barren world, it seemed. A spattering of dun grasses, over which a cold wind was blowing, added to my discomfort. The water was a greenish-gray and came thundering in with ten-foot-high waves. Spray from those waves was drenching my cablestitch sweater. My hip-length boots had been running wet for hours.

Where the hell was that girl?

My name is Rod Damon. I am a sociology professor at a big university, and the founder of the League for Sexual Dynamics. I am also a member of the Thaddeus X. Coxe Foundation, which is an espionage establishment operating more or less independently of everybody except its boss, whom I know only as Walrus-moustache. Who he reports to is absolutely unknown to me, possibly as a security measure. It is enough for me to report to him. He is something else again; he might have modeled for the original ogre.

I cursed him under my breath as I made a cast, sending the bare hook and the lead sinker out about fifty yards. My reel made a nice, whirring sound which would have been music to my lonesome ears if there'd been a bit of bait on that hook to attract one of the big bluefish that converge along the seventy-odd miles of unspoiled beach here at the Outer Banks off the coast of North Carolina.

This was his idea—that I should be out here freezing to death and pretending to fish. One of our Coxe Foundation agents had made a big catch himself: he had tied onto an agent for the Opposition, and from him—with the help of truth drug or two—the Old Man had learned that something big was in the wind.

The man our boy in Raleigh had come up with was a paid assassin. A professional killer. They do exist, you know; you rarely hear of them because they are pretty smart cookies, they are never seen. The deaths they cause appear to be accidental ones. There is rarely any reason to suspect murder.

The Foundation knew somebody wanted a man killed. Otherwise, why employ a killer-for-hire? The question we wanted to find out the answer to was: Who was marked for death, and why?

This was my job, to get that answer.

So here I was, reeling in a wet line with an empty hook and cursing the Fates who had made me a secret agent responsible only to Walrus-moustache. He was sleeping the sound slumber of those with unspotted conscience, while I——

"Hi!" a voice bubbled. "I'm Laura Ogden."

I turned my head and forgot to move the reel handle. A girl was walking across the sand, a big friendly smile on her gorgeous face. She wore a sweater under which her body must have been naked, because her ample breasts jiggled and shook with over ripe enthusiasm at her every sand-kicking step. Below the French-knit beige sweater with its low-cut cowl neck, her curving hips were held by a pair of hip-huggers that revealed the fact she wore a bikini panty under them. The dark brown hip-huggers were tight to her thighs and knees; under them, she showed lithe,

6

long legs. There were red leather beach sandals on her otherwise bare feet.

"Hi, yourself," I grinned.

She came right up to me, head cocked to one side so her brown hair could spill down over one shoulder. She had brown eyes, and her mouth was daubed with a brilliant shade of red lipstick.

"Catch anything?" she asked softly.

"I'll make a killing yet," I responded.

These were the passwords, as reported by the paid killer our man in Raleigh had captured. I had not seen him, though I knew his name was Albert Frame. I just hoped he had been telling the truth.

Her smile dazzled me, it welcomed me to the club. She put out her right hand, I gave it a clasp and smiled back at her.

"Where do we go?" I wondered, waving my free hand at the beach to indicate this was one of the most God-forsaken spots I had ever seen, especially at this time of year.

"Oh, not too far," she answered, letting go of my hand and turning so I could take a gander at her behind cheeks in the tight hip-huggers. I looked, and was impressed. She appeared to frown when I stared at her plump buttocks, but in a moment her face was bland, except for the faint smile.

I reeled in my line. I said, "Oh, damn. I lost my bait." I fitted the hook to the line, bent and picked up a bait box and a short-handled net, as well as my small knapsack, and a green metal fishing tackle box.

She was striding about ten feet ahead of me, glancing back over her shoulder. It seemed to me she was putting a little extra sexiness in her walk, because her buttocks jiggled somewhat more than they should have. I looked at them with appreciation. They were exciting buttocks. I know, because it was exciting *me*.

True, I am afflicted with priapism. This means I am almost perpetually in heat, with my manhood constantly at attention. It takes very little to set me off, just the sight of a jiggling plump behind or a pair of breasts naked under a

7

thin cashmere sweater—like now, with this lovely brunette on this lonely beach.

She slowed her walk so I could catch up.

I saw her eyes move to the front of my rather tight slacks. I was wearing an old pair for the fishing bit, and maybe they were too worn, too tight, because she got that frown on her face again—a look of deep puzzlement, as if she could not understand how she could excite any man this way. So she tucked her arm in mine, rubbing her breast against my arm and gave me a really sultry look.

"You know, I didn't expect to find anybody as handsome as you," she cooed. "I've never seen Albert Frame before—his name was recommended to us by a mutual friend—but I admit I'd preconceived you in my mind. Somebody small and mean and sneaky, with pale blue eyes and thin blonde hair, that was how I thought you'd be. Instead, you're a regular he-man."

I grinned. "I do my best."

She hugged me even tighter to her softness. "Midge will be glad to see you. Midge is very hard up at the moment."

"Ah? And who is Midge?"

"My companion. We work in pairs, you know."

"Do I?"

Her laughter rang out. "Not really. You don't know any more about us than we do about you, isn't that right? All our mutual friend did was set up the meeting and provide us with the passwords so we'd know each other at our rendezvous point."

This jibed with what the real Albert Frame had told Walrus-moustache when he had been interrogated. The boss had passed on the info to me when he'd told me I was going to become Albert Frame.

The Old Man had added that I did not look like Frame, I was bigger and stronger, but I did have eyes, ears, nose and brown hair, so he figured I would pass. Besides, the girls had never laid eyes on Albert Frame.

I passed all right. My brunette beauty kept nudging her heavy breast into my arm and giggling at sight of my reaction. She seemed to be getting an unholy delight from the

8

fact that I was all man and obviously responsive to her charms.

There was a tan Ford Fairlane parked on the one main road that runs along this length of beachland, from Whalebone Junction to Ocracoke. We headed for it with my girlfriend glancing at me inquiringly.

"Where's your car?" she wondered.

"I took a taxi from Nag's Head," I lied. Actually it had been a Coxe Foundation car—disguised as a taxi, it is true—that had delivered me to the lonely beach designated as a rendezvous point by Albert Frame. I added, "It wasn't necessary to have him come back to pick me up. I figured on meeting you."

She nodded, quite satisfied.

I stowed my gear in the trunk, took off my wading boots, and made myself more or less presentable in my rugged sweater, my old slacks, and a pair of Hush Puppies I removed from my knapsack. Then I slid in beside my girl guide and let her take me where we could be alone.

She drove with competence, handling the Ford with the delicate touch of a Mickey Thompson rocketing his Challenger along the Bonneville Salt Flats. Her eyes were turned straight ahead and she gave me no more glances. It was almost as if she had forgotten my existence.

To make conversation, I murmured, "These Outer Banks are chockful of history, you know. Sir Walter Raleigh founded a colony here, the first English settlement in America. This was the same Roanoke Colony from which the second group of colonists vanished without a trace. The first batch went back to England, it was such an inhospitable place."

"I always thought that colony was on the mainland, for some reason," she murmured, giving me a swift glance before her eyes went back to the road.

"No, it was here, not too far from Kitty Hawk, where the Wright brothers made the first airplane flight. There's always a good, stiff breeze blowing somewhere around these Banks."

"Like a hurricane," she laughed.

"The strongest hurricane of them all blew away the

9

wind-velocity machines from Cape Hatteras weather station more than twenty years ago. Nobody knows how strong that blow was, but it was estimated at a hundred and ten miles an hour."

"You're a regular encyclopedia," she murmured. "I didn't know paid killers were so learned."

"We have a lot of time on our hands between jobs. One has to do something. I soak up a lot of trivia."

"Tell me more," she cajoled.

I babbled more trivia because I was puzzled by my brunette companion and I wanted to cover up the searching glances I kept giving her. She appeared to be equally puzzled by me, for some reason I couldn't figure out, as if she knew something about me I did not, and was perturbed by it.

I couldn't even guess what was troubling her, Albert Frame had been insistent on the fact that he had never seen the girls and they had never seen him, not even his picture. At last I told myself I was just imagining things.

I went on talking a little longer. Then I saw Laura putting a sandaled foot on the brake and turning the wheel. We were some miles past Kill Devil Hill, moving on a small narrow dirt road winding in between oak trees and holly bushes, then along a narrow lane where I caught glimpses of a white picket fence from time to time.

We drove a few miles more, into what seemed to be a forest. There couldn't be any houses around here. This corner of the world was wild and remote, even for the Outer Banks. Yet, there was a house here, a small building of two storys and twin dormers, I saw when the car finally stopped. Its grayish, weatherbeaten shingles curled slightly, to add a touch of strange beauty to the beach cottage, half hidden behind a fence and some stunted oak trees.

Laura Ogden had braked in a rutted driveway.

She smiled at me and waved her hand at the house. "Thar she blows, Albert. Our little hideout. We can talk safely enough in there. Nobody will overhear us, you can bet on that. We're three miles from nowhere, out this far."

"You picked a real good place," I complimented her,

sliding out to stretch my legs and fasten the details of this hideaway more firmly in my mind. The Foundation would want to know where it was and how its agents could get here to liquidate any members of the Opposition who might still be using it for a hideout, after I'd found out what Walrus-moustache wanted to know.

Laura and her plump behind was moving along a flagstoned path toward a colonial front door with a fanlight over it and glass panes on either side. I went after her.

As her forefinger touched a bell, I heard chimes.

A blonde answered the door, looking at Laura and past her at me. Her blue eyes widened in what I took for surprise.

"Here's Albert, Midge," Laura said. "Albert, meet Midge Priest."

Midge was wearing a wrapper, a bathrobe, which with her damp hair pushed up into a golden mop atop her shapely head suggested that she had just come from the bath. Her left hand held the robe together at her chest. A rope belt kept it closed around her midsection.

"Hi there, Albert," Midge said, but she was looking at Laura, as if trying to read some unspoken message in her eyes.

"Glad to meet you, Midge," I said, grinning and holding out my hand. She took her right hand from the doorknob to take it. Her face showed worry, I thought.

"Albert's quite a man," Laura snickered, halting in the little hallway and turning to glance at me.

"Oh?" Midge looked even more worried. "How so?"

"Show her, Albert."

I laughed. "Hey, this isn't part of the deal."

Laura Ogden giggled. "Of course it isn't. I just thought you might like a little fun before we get down to the serious business."

Midge said weakly, "But I thought——"

The brunette gestured airily, "You thought I was too devoted to the Cause to bother about such things as love-ins, didn't you? Well, I'm not. Not when there's somebody like Albert around. Come on, Midge, take off the robe and

11

let Albert see what a doll you are."

Midge stared from Laura to me and back again. Her shoulders lifted and fell and her breasts moved behind the light wrapper. I looked at them and started to get a rise out of them.

Laura hooted, "You see? You see?"

Midge saw, staring hard at my too-tight slacks. The yeast was rising fast. Midge whistled softly, and her eyes got bright. "Yeah," she exclaimed softly, "I catch what you mean, Laura. He is a one, isn't he?"

Her hand fell away from its clutch on the lapels of her bathrobe. The lapels parted, showing that as far down as her belly button, Midge Priest was all girl. I could see the inner slopes of large white breasts to the circles of her red nipples. I could also make out faint blue veins under the taut white flesh.

Laura said, "I don't know about you, Midge, but I've been a good girl for too long a time. Seeing Albert there has started a fire in my forest."

The blonde girl chuckled, moving on bare feet toward a record player and bending over it to slide a record onto its spindle, taking her time. Maybe she knew that the thin fabric outlined her buttocks and she was letting me get an eyeful of their shapeliness.

When she turned from the phonograph she held her arms out and bumped her hips from side to side. "Do you dance, Albert?" she wondered out loud.

I stepped into her arms, caught her middle and we did a swing around the room while Laura applauded from the hall arch. She watched us for a few minutes, then said casually that she would whip together some sandwiches and a drink.

The music changed to a fast bugaloo beat. Midge stepped back and went into the jerky rhythm, arms pumping. The action sent those flaps back even further, making them wave about, revealing the big naked breasts behind them that leaped and bobbed to her movements. She laughed when she noticed my interest.

"I think Laura is a kind of genius, don't you? I mean,

12

finding you like that and you turning out this way. We can have fun, man."

Midge came closer, bending over a little so I could see all the way to her creamy belly and dimpled navel. Tiny devils danced in her eyes. When the music stopped, she jammed her softness up against me, fastening her arms about my neck and bumped her mons veneris against my manhood.

Her open mouth caught my lips.

When we started to break apart, Laura joined us, offering her own ripe lips to my mouth. I felt her wet tongue slither between my lips for a few seconds while her hand found its way down my front to where my libido had its living quarters.

"Mmmmm-hmmmm!" she breathed, squeezing.

"Being randy is dandy," I managed to gasp, "but don't you think we ought to get down to business? After all, I have to earn my keep by killing, you know."

"Now, don't be a spoilsport," Midge smiled up into my face, shaking her head as her nimble fingers began sliding combs and hairpins out of her golden mop. Her yellow tresses started coming loose. On my other side, Laura Ogden was grinning wickedly.

"Which one of us gets him?" she was asking.

"Me," stated Midge, cudding my left leg between her thighs, her right arm hooked about my lean waist. "I need him more than you do. I've been cooped up on that isl—"

She broke off, looking guilty. I leaned to kiss the tip of her nose. "There's plenty to go around," I assured her. "I have a thing going for me. Priapism."

Laura blinked. "What's that?"

"I'm a phallic perpetual motion machine. I never run down or out of fuel. I just keep chugging along."

Midge let her eyes go wide. "That on the level?"

Laura murmured, "How can it be? Act your age, Midge."

"I'll prove it," I promised them. "Who's going to be first?"

Midge whispered, "Me!"

13

Laura shrugged, a wicked glint in her eyes. "All right, you take Midge. I'll—er—keep busy while you're wriggling navels."

Midge was shaking her shoulders back and forth. Her bold eyes were fastened on my face so she could read my stupefied admiration as I stared at her jiggling breasts, her smoothly mounded belly and the fluffy golden fleece at her loins. A tiny voice whispered in my mind that she was coming on strong—too strong to be natural.

She let the robe trail to the floor. Her thighs were soft, untanned, and the curving calves and dimpled knees added to her amoral attractiveness. Maybe she was a nympho, I told myself. I had had experience with nymphomaniacs in my work as founder and teacher of L.S.D. I could sympathize with them, since in a sense, with my priapism, I was a male nympho myself.

I drew Midge by a hand toward a sofa. I said, "This isn't going to be any quickie bout, honey. You deserve only my best efforts."

Midge beamed as I kissed her soft shoulder, then ran my lips down her spine to the cleavage of her buttocks. While I was doing that, my fingers were busy yanking off my turtleneck sweater, unbuckling my belt and sliding down my pants. My hands carried my jockey shorts right along with them.

I heard Laura gasp as she stared.

I might be going under the name of Albert Frame, but it was as Rod Damon, founder of the League for Sexual Dynamics, that I made my appearance. I took a step forward and began my tick-tack task. My tongue slid around on creamy skin, as Midge oohed and shivered. My fingertips ran all around her softly fleshed hips. I knelt down behind her.

"I'll build a jump suit of kisses for you, Midge," I murmured, using my lips in that manner which the Hindu erotologists named the Coral and the Jewel, "all over your divine flesh."

My teeth and my lips joined in the tribute I paid to her beauty. Each plump cheek was a meadow on which to browse like a lamb scrabbling for goodies. Midge was

14

shaking pretty much by the time my Coral and Jewel kisses had gone down her thighs to the backs of her knees. My mouth could feel her trembling.

I turned her and kissed up her body in front.

Her head was flung back, her eyes were closed and her red lips were parted to aid the hurried breathing which shook her breasts. On either side of her rounded hips, her hands had formed fists, to help her control her emotions.

When I got to the golden fleece, she could not restrain her wail of ecstasy. I burrowed deeper, she screamed thickly as I played the part of Eunus to Phyllis, as Ausonius has related in his Epigrams. I formed the delta, the psi and the lambda with my tongue and her flesh.

I was not finished, but Midge was. She shook and convulsed, bending above me with her head down so low her long blonde hair brushed across my spine. Her voice screamed out the intensity of her pleasure.

I let her fall back onto the couch. On a foot and one knee, I lunged forward, my palms sliding up her underthighs to catch her buttocks. Together, we formed the *el asemeud* of the Arab world, with her thighs pressed backward against her breasts by my weight even while my hands gripped her shoulders.

Five minutes went by, ten minutes.

Midge was a blonde bomb exploding in a series of catastrophic convulsions as I went on being Rod Damon. My pride had been stung a bit by Laura Ogden; I was determined to show her and Midge that my every word was a true one. I think Midge fainted after a time.

At any rate, Laura was grabbing my arm and trying to yank me free. She was cursing, sobbing and yelling that I was killing her friend. I think she was jealous, because when I whirled on her and her eyes fell to my groin, a red flush tinted her cheeks.

"Get those slacks off," I panted.

She tried to slap my face but I am an expert in judo, karate and other assorted forms of mayhem which include the art of self-defense. I brushed her right wrist aside with my left, with my right hand I grabbed her French-knit sweater and yanked.

15

Laura screeched, "You'll ruin it!"

She tried to fight but I was far too strong for her. I had the cowl-neck sweater up and half off one arm before she realized what I was doing. My lips went to the wobbling breast nearest my mouth. My weight bore her back onto the hook rug.

Her hands tried to push my head away.

This left my own hands free to work on her slacks. I got them down her milky thighs, I pushed one leg free. It waved around in midair before I could tighten my grip on her bumping hips. The fight went out of her as I went in.

She panted as her eyes blazed fire at me, but her female flesh was betraying her. She had watched me with Midge, she wanted a piece of the action. Now she had it and she knew damn well what to do with it. Her hips lifted and swung, looped and rolled. She was touching the floor with her heels and the back of her head. She was engaging in the feminime response known as "the juicing of the orange."

Her position—cramped between me and the floor, on her heels and head—prevented her from fully enjoying this movement in which the orange half is likened to the female organ and the squeezer bulb to the male. So I caught her up in my arms, lifting her off the floor and walked with her to a straight-backed chair. I planted my rump and let her rest on my thighs so her toes could touch the floor for support.

She had her eyes closed all this time. When she felt my arms drop away to free her hips, she opened them and glared at me. Her lips were contorted grotesquely as she panted words at me.

"Damn you! Damn you! I'm going to drain you and then I'm going to kill you! Do you understand that? I'm going to kill you and—"

She was making talk to help delay her orgasmic reaction to her situation, I figured. I was wrong. I found out later she meant it.

Right now I just let her do her diddling dance while watching her heavy breasts swing and sway before me. Her face was a mirror reflecting the inner turmoil of her

16

all-girl parts. Laura Ogden was engaged in a tail-wagging tantrum that lifted her psyche up and into the Elysian Fields, so anything she said was not to be believed.

I had her figured for the kind of a female who talks and talks and talks even while engaging in erotic exercise. Just goes to show that even a sexpert like myself can make a mistake now and then.

Finally she slumped against me, soft and warm and wet with sweat. My arms cradled her gently. She moaned, knowing my manhood was still in its criomediac condition.

"Well? Believe me now?" I asked gently.

"I do," said Midge, standing beside me, starting to push Laura off her perch. "Come on, come on! I want another whack of that!"

"It's time for business," Laura stated.

"Buttonhole business," Midge snapped. "Now climb off!"

She pushed Laura so that the brunette had to step down to maintain her balance. Instantly Midge was taking her place, swinging a leg over my lap and dropping right on target. She smiled in delight, settling herself with a wicked wrench of her hips, then leaning forward to kiss the tip of my nose with her parted lips.

"No rush, honey," she breathed. "You took the bite out of me. I can go nice and easy now. No sweat."

We went nice and easy for a while. Then Midge began to pant and buck and jump. "My God, you aren't for real," she sobbed, going into a violent climax.

"You can say that again," Laura snapped tartly.

I lifted my eyes, staring over a bare white shoulder at Laura Ogden. Except for her high-heeled shoes, she was standing there before me stark naked. She made a very interesting sight.

Especially since she had a gun in her hand.

The gun was aimed at me—the best part of me.

CHAPTER TWO

I blinked a couple of times, but the gun was still there. It did not weave; it was as steady as a rock. My first instinct was to push Midge away and make a dive for the Smith and Wesson.

I managed to control myself. Laura Ogden did not look as if she could possibly miss at such a distance. She was five feet away. And the thought of a .32 bullet ploughing into my flesh was not at all appetizing. So I kept my hands on the white hips I was holding and made back and forth motions with them, causing Midge to whimper and move her haunches the way I wanted.

She came to life, straightening up and swinging her hips like a hula dancer. I was still looking at Laura, trying to read her expression.

"Why the gun?" I asked.

Midge was startled. She turned her head, saw Laura and the blue-steel revolver. "No, Laura—not yet! Not yet, goddamnit!"

So my blonde *boussole* was in on this scheme to get rid of me. It did not lessen my desire, knowing this, but it did change the trend of my thinking. I had two women to overcome, not just one.

"Why?" I asked.

"You aren't Albert Frame."

"Of course I am!" I asserted, my heart sinking.

My premonitions, built on the puzzled looks Laura Ogden had given me and the speed with which Midge Priest had thrown her nakedness at my maleness, were coming true. The girls, with some sort of feminine in-

18

tuition, had guessed at the truth.

Laura Ogden gave a wicked smile. "Then if you are, Albert Frame has changed his habits, his entire personality."

The longer I could keep her talking, the better off I would be. "How come? I thought you'd never seen me before."

"I never have. I was only told one thing about you by our mutual acquaintance. That the real Albert Frame is a fag, a queen, a fairy. He could no more be aroused by women than this gun. Catch wise, mister? It was our only way to know the real Albert Frame."

Midge was whimpering, "Not yet, Laura. Oh, not yet!"

The Thaddeus X. Coxe Foundation is a pretty thorough organization, generally speaking. This time they had goofed by not discovering one little fact about the man I was pretending to be. If I ever saw Walrus-moustache again, I would suggest a few improvements to be made in his methods of interrogation. Especially when I was involved in the situation.

It didn't look as if I'd ever see the Old Man again, however. So if I was going to get out of this squeeze, it was up to me.

"Our mutual friend lied to you," I said.

"Why should he do that?"

"He—ah—was jealous of me. I—ah—stole his girl friend."

Laura hooted. "Our mutual friend is a girl, dummy!"

"Right! She's a lesbian."

"Nice try, whoever you are, but it just won't wash. Hurry up, Midge! For God's sake, haven't you had enough yet?"

"I can never get enough of this wonderful man. Laura, do we have to kill him? I mean, he's like a treasure. And what a treasure! Oooooh! *Oooooooh!*"

Midge was catapulting into a frenzy.

I took advantage of the fact that Laura took her eyes off me long enough to stare at her spy buddy, to tighten my fingers in the naked hips flailing away at me. I dug my fingertips deep into soft female flesh. Then I hoisted her

19

off and flung her through the air at Laura.

The brunette squawked in surprise as Midge slammed into her. Both girls toppled, slamming onto the floor. I was right behind them, diving off the chair in a long, low arc that brought me down on top of naked girl-flesh with a resounding thump.

My left hand went for the gun. I wrapped fingers around it, I yanked at it. Laura had her finger wrapped about the trigger. The gun went off almost in my face. Luckily, the barrel was pointing at the far wall at the time. My hand wrenched, the gun came free, and I hurled the Smith and Wesson through the window. The glass pane gave way with a satisfying crash. The last I saw of that revolver, it was headed for a clump of bushes.

Midge kicked me in the belly and the wind went out of me.

Tears were streaming down her face and she was sobbing like a sick calliope. "I ha-hate to d-do this, ho-honey," she wept, but her bare foot kicked me again, right smack in the solar plexus.

I felt like being sick, but I didn't dare. I had to overcome these females or let them kill me. I lunged, grabbing Midge where her pain would be the worst when my fingers tightened. I made contact. I made pain. Midge screamed, both hands on my wrist, trying to dislodge my grip on her femininity.

"Laura! Stop him! Oh my God, get him off!"

Laura tried. She leaped and her hands plunged for my male equipment to pay me back in kind. I raised my left knee. Her face ran into it, hard. She shrieked and forgot my manhood to put her hands to her face. I saw blood streaming from her nose just as I launched myself at Midge. The blonde was scrambling to her feet, and I got a fast look at her jellying white buttocks and a long pale leg an instant before she whirled and kicked.

I was too weak to avoid that foot. The wind was out of my lungs, my muscles felt like water. My neck would still work, so I turned my head. But not fast enough. Midge rammed her heel into the side of my jaw.

20

The leg muscles are a hell of a lot stronger than the arm muscles. I could let Midge hammer my jaw all day long with her fist without minding it too much. Her leg was something else. Her bare heel was like the fist of a Jack Dempsey; it rocked me back on the floor, half out of my skull. I gasped and flopped, trying to get up.

Laura was as mad as the proverbial wet hen by this time. With blood flowing from her nostrils, she landed with both knees on my middle. This time I went flopping like a gaffed fish, unable to breathe, unable to stop her hands from clawing at my delicacy.

I heard Midge yell, "Not there!"

Something hit my thigh and I was dimly aware of Midge wrestling with Laura, trying to prevent her from really ruining me as a man. Laura was sobbing, panting harshly; Midge was weeping with the tears running down her cheeks.

More wrestling sounds, more panting. Then Laura must have quieted down, because when she spoke, it was in a more normal voice.

"All right, you win. But we've still got to kill him."

"I su-suppose so. But it's such a waste!"

There were some more words. I never heard them. I was floating in a kind of stupor right about then. Midge's heel had really popped me. I felt myself being lifted by the heels and dragged with my head dragging along the floor, out of the living room and into the kitchen.

"He's heavy," Midge panted.

"Yeah. We'll just push him through the cellar door and let him go the rest of the way by gravity."

"Don't you have any heart at all?"

"Sure I do, but he's out cold, he won't feel anything."

Somebody opened a door and I felt a draft. Then the girls were pushing me through the open door. My head felt a stair tread, then I was turning over slowly and starting my downward fall.

"One more time," Midge gasped.

"Wander wherever you will—here we come!" Laura snapped.

My body seemed to take wings. It practically flew down the stairs. By the time I hit the cellar floor, I was far out beyond the world. I had passed out.

I thought I was dead when I opened my eyes. I was in utter darkness, there wasn't a light anywhere. And all my senses were reeling. I hung between earth and heaven for what seemed an eternity. Heaven was a place of celestial music with angels flying around, I told myself in a dim corner of my mind, so I was not in Heaven.

And Hell was a red flame of fire, with devils holding pitchforks. I gathered that I was not in Hell.

Limbo, then! Limbo is a place of exterior darkness.

But did Limbo smell? Of gas?

I could suddenly hear the hissing sound. The stench was even stronger. I groaned and rolled over. I was on the cellar floor and my wrists and ankles were tied. There was a gas burner somewhere around here, probably used to heat water, and the valve was open.

I crawled across the cellar. The stone floor was like ice on my naked flesh, but there was a little starlight outside—it was night, right enough—and the starlight plus my night vision enabled me to make out dim shapes.

I was trying not to breathe, of course. I was sick enough without taking in any more gas from the metal bottle somewhere outside the cottage. I made it to my knees, which were not tied. I crawled around that damn cellar for what seemed to be forever, but which couldn't have been more than a few minutes.

My head found the water heater by bumping into it. I turned my back and sat down with my spine resting against the tank. My wrists were tied together, but I could still fumble around with my fingers.

So I fumbled around until I located the shut-off valve and turned it. The hissing stopped but the cellar was still full of gas. I fell over on my side and wanted to be sick. I knew I was going to pass out, and that maybe the gas already in the cellar would be enough to finish me off.

I didn't dare enjoy the luxury of sickness. I had to find a window and open it so the clean night air could come in

22

here and revive me. I leaned against the water heater and made it to my feet. I hopped around to the small cellar window, high in the wall and close to the ceiling. With my wrists tied, I could never open its catch.

I hopped to the window and found I could stare out at the bushes and the stars. I could also see a helicopter hovering about the house.

At sight of that whirlybird, my heart began hammering. Good old Walrus-moustache! When I didn't report in, he'd sent some Foundation agents to find me. The lights were still on in the house; that meant that our two birds had not yet flown the coop. I practically danced up and down in my delight.

Then I saw the girls running across the lawn, waving up at the chopper craft. So much for my happy thoughts about the Old Man. This was an Opposition whirlybird. It would land and pick up the girls and there went our chance to find out who was going to get killed.

But the helicopter did not land. It hovered in the air about a hundred feet above the lawn. Instead—The girls began rising. They went up side by side, levitating as easily as I was standing there gaping at them. I looked for wings. I searched their shapely bodies for some sort of flying rocket belt, a la Buck Rogers. No wings, no rocket belt. No nothing but their girlish bodies in mod clothes.

Midge was wearing a belt dress with black leather boots and a leather helmet for her golden hair. Laura had on bell-bottomed slacks and a matching tunic, with a silver pendant around her neck. No balloons were attached to them either, other than their natural attributes as well-developed females. No, sir. They were just lifting upward, smiling and looking up at the helicopter.

Magic! It had to be magic or else I was so filled with gas I was hallucinating here in the cellar with my nose poked against the window glass. Yeah, like on lysergic acid diethylamide (also known as LSD). I was damn sure I wasn't on a hallucinogen, however. Things like pot and speed and LSD are not my bag.

My jaw was open as I watched Midge and Laura hover like angels near that chopper craft. The light coming from an upper-story window framed them so neatly there was absolutely no mistake about it. I was not having visions. Those girls had levitated the way Friar Joseph of Copertino is reported to have levitated, just rising upward into the air in defiance of gravity.

An instant later they were in and the whirlybird glided sideways and off into the sheltering darkness. I stood there gawking, not believing my eyes.

I slammed the glass with my forehead. I hit that pane a good smack. The glass shattered and cut my forehead, but the cool night air wafted in and I leaned against the cellar wall and breathed it in.

My head was in reasonably good working order by the time I knelt down and fumbled around for a piece of broken window pane. I managed by trial and error to cut through the cord that held my wrists. I cut my fingers in half a dozen places before I freed myself, but when my hands were loose, it was easy to get my legs back in working order.

I stood on my tiptoes and managed to get my head through the window without slashing my neck. I bellowed, I yelled, I shouted.

Only the nighttime darkness heard me.

This house was in a remote part of the Outer Banks. I could have used a bull-horn and not have been heard by anybody. I thought about the cellar door. Maybe I was being a damn fool, standing here and roaring, when all I had to do was go open the cellar door.

Rather sheepishly, I stumbled around until I found the cellar stairs and mounted them. The door was locked. I spent fifteen minutes trying to slam a shoulder into that door and open it the way they do in the movies. All I got out of it was a bruised shoulder.

I sat down on the top step and tried to think. There must be a way out. The door was impenetrable, the cellar window was too small for me to squeeze through. My voice was too weak to carry very far.

I sagged into the wall, sweating and half nauseous. The gas inside me was getting to my inner man. I felt like retching.

24

An hour later, I heard Walrus-moustache yelling my name. More hallucinations!

"Damon, have you gone deaf?"

"Funny," I said out loud. "That sounds just like the Chief."

"It had better damn well sound like the Chief because it is the Chief, you nincompoop! Now come away from that corner over to this window."

I turned and stared. The Old Man had his face down there at the level of the window, peering in at me. I heard him say, "Dammit, where the hell's that flashlight? Somebody get me a flashlight, dammit."

"No need, Chief," I laughed. "I'm on my way."

I was halfway to the window when my legs got all rubbery. I found myself sinking down on that cold stone floor, aware only of a vast surprise. This sort of thing had never happened to me before. Then I lost touch with the world.

I came to in Heaven. I knew where I was, all right. An angel was smiling down at me and soothing my forehead with a perfumed palm. Do angels smell of Chanel perfume? And wear nurse's caps perched atop bright red hair? This angel did.

"All right, all right," growled the Old Man, moving in on my Florence Nightingale. "Can he hear me?"

"Yes, sir. He can hear you."

The Chief stuck his face in front of the nurse so I was ogling him. "Get that stupid look off your face, Damon," he shouted.

"Yes, sir, Chief," I gulped.

"What the hell happened to you?"

"I was damn near murdered in cold blood," I shouted back, "all on account of you!"

His shocked face restored some of my confidence. I slid a hand sideways so my fingertips touched the redheaded nurse on her palm. I let my fingernails tickle it. The redhead hid a smile behind her free hand but did not draw her palm away.

"On account of me?"

"Next time you interrogate a prisoner, find out if he's a

25

normal man or not! The only thing those girls knew about him was that he's a homo."

The Chief groaned. The nurse looked interested.

"Oh, no," Walrus-moustache muttered. "Not again. Why did you have to play games with them?"

"They tempted me, Chief," I remarked virtuously, "and you know how quickly and—ah—strongly I react to temptation."

The nurse was squeezing my finger between her soft, pink digits. There was a delightful look in her brown eyes.

Walrus-moustache growled, "I don't suppose you learned anything?"

"Nothing," I murmured.

"Then how are you going to stop a murder?"

"I'm sure I can't tell you," I answered, lost in the brown eyes beaming down at me as the nurse went on soothing my forehead. "Since I didn't even learn who was going to get killed, the how and why of it needn't concern us."

"Young lady—get lost!" thundered Walrus-moustache.

My redheaded nurse looked startled, and scared. "Y-yes, sir," she gasped and rose to her feet. She ran from the room. I gazed after her shapely legs under the mini-skirted uniform before I turned on my case officer.

"What's the idea?" I howled. "I'm a sick man!"

"Damon, you aren't taking this situation seriously."

"I am, I am! But what can I do?"

"You can begin by thinking."

"Oh, I'm thinking, all right, Chief."

"About this case you're on—not about the nurse."

The Chief was right. I was not thinking about the case. But what in hell was there to think about? I had seen two girls rise upward into the air and step into a chopper craft. The helicopter had cut out for parts unknown. Big deal!

"You should have seen them," I muttered dreamily. "They flew right up into the air. It was scary."

"What the hell are you talking about, Damon?"

I told him about the girls levitating. He told me I was nuts.

"Dammit, I know what I saw. Go outside if you don't

26

believe me, around to one side of the house, to the south. You may see their footprints there. Those footprints will end abruptly where they took off for that helicopter."

"Sure, sure," Walrus-moustache soothed me.

"Then the whirlybird flew north," I went on.

Walrus-moustache snorted. He was badly disturbed.

"Just a hint, a hint," he pleaded. He seemed to have forgotten all about the levitating females. Obviously he thought I'd been imagining the whole thing.

Nothing came to me. I shrugged and looked helpless.

"Oh, hell!" shouted the Chief. "Go on back to your motel."

I felt a little sorry for him. He could not even lecture me, because he had nothing to lecture about, other than the fact that I had goofed. And it was not so much my goof as it had been that of the Foundation boys who had interrogated Albert Frame. He could not appeal to my patriotism, because nobody knew whether patriotism was involved in the murder we were not going to prevent.

He took another look at me and shrugged.

"Okay, okay—you look pretty sick," he admitted. "Miss Kolb! Where the hell's that nurse?" He scowled at me. "So I'd better make sure you live through the night. I'll send her along to play doctor for you."

The redhead came back fearfully.

"Miss Kolb, you'd better go with him," he told her. "I don't want anything happening to him. He needs rest and medicines. You know what to do. Stay with him for a day or two, then phone me. I'll try and come up with some solution to the case by that time."

The nurse bent over the sofa, her brown eyes wistful. "Do you think you can get up by yourself? And walk? Or shall I call for a stretcher?"

I slid my right arm about her waist. "Just give me a hand, honey. The old professor is a little weak, but I'm not out yet."

I made it to my feet and walked about the room leaning on Miss Kolb, my arm around her middle. She was soft female flesh, all perfumed, and I felt her thigh nudge mine as we walked, and the brush of her curved hip.

27

"Damon, have you got a tape recorder?" the boss-man asked.

"Sure, Chief."

"All right, this is what I want you to do when you get to your motel room. Without fail, mind! I want you to get in bed—alone!—and talk into that recorder. Tell it everything that happened to you, everything you did and said, everything those girls did and said. Understand?"

"Everything?" I asked weakly.

Walrus-moustache glanced at Miss Kolb. He muttered, "Miss Kolb is a nurse. She'll understand. Maybe something—a dropped word, a phrase, anything like that—will hit your memory cells. It may furnish us with a clue as to who those women mean to murder. We have to know, Damon. We—must—know!"

"Right, Chief," I nodded.

My body was discovering that it was not nearly as strong as my mind believed it to be. I got dizzy, so dizzy I would have fallen if Walrus-moustache hadn't jumped to my left side to help the redhead keep me on my feet.

"He's worse off than I thought," I heard him say. "Let him stay here. Put him into a bed in one of the upstairs rooms. You stay with him, nurse. I'll leave a man on guard down here, to make sure you're both all right. I'll stay at a hotel in Manns Harbor."

I leaned back against the sofa. I passed out.

I came to in a bed in a small bedroom dimly lighted by a small lamp on a night table. I opened my eyes to the face of a bearded man sitting beside the bed, a hypodermic in his hand. Just beyond him I made out my redheaded nurse. She looked worried.

"That ought to bring him around," murmured the doctor. "He needed rest; he's had it and we can begin feeding him."

Whatever was in that hypodermic worked like magic.

In ten minutes, I was feeling myself again, I opened my mouth and bellowed. Moments later I heard footsteps on the stairs and on the hall floorboards. Then Miss Kolb stood in the doorway, beaming at me.

"You're better," she said. "I'm so glad. You had us all

28

worried for a while. But the doctor was just here, he said you'll come along fine now. I'll go boil a couple of eggs for you. With toast and coffee."

I ate my meal with the redhead seated on the edge of the mattress, hand-feeding me. There was a tape recorder downstairs for me to play with as soon as I ate my breakfast, she informed me. It had come yesterday, with the compliments of Walrus-moustache.

"Yesterday? How long've I been here?"

"You passed out on us day before yesterday. You've been asleep ever since. The doctor said it was the best thing that could've happened to you."

I digested that as I digested my food.

Two whole days lost. Those girls might have already zeroed in on their victim. If they had, there wasn't anything I could do. But on the off-chance that they had not, that they had been delayed for one reason or another—

"I guess you'd better bring the recorder up here," I admitted with a wry grin. "I'd hate to think somebody was killed on account of some slip-up of mine."

Miss Kolb beamed and patted my hand.

Ten minutes later I was putting down words on tape. I told the whole story, leaving out nothing. It ended with my being pushed down the cellar stairs.

As an afterthought, I told how I had turned off the gas, how I had broken the window, and saw these two flying fleshpots rise up into the air.

This was the unexpurgated edition, which I would erase from the tape later on. I would provide Walrus-moustache with a censored version but first I wanted to see if anything in our sexual antics could clue me in about Midge and Laura.

I ran the tape back, listening intently. Nothing. In disgust I shut off the damn thing and lay there, thinking. Thinking was no better than listening, as far as inspiration went, so I yelled for Miss Kolb and asked for a paper.

I lay there and read the entire paper. Even the society pages caught my eye. Debutante Martha Therese Walcott was marrying Emmet Hazelton of Edenton, Harriet Gail Oddsley was divorcing her husband whom she had found

29

in bed with two women. Wanda Weaver Yule, the former rodeo star and widow of financier Harold Hayes Yule, was injured in a freak accident when her car motor exploded. Helena Mae Thurwood was visiting her grandchildren in Charlotte. All the local news that's fit to print.

I got bored, after a time.

I thought about the fact that all Southern women had two names instead of one, and used them all the time. The men too. Names like Billy Joe, Eddie John, Jimmy Lou. I wondered why, but I had no answer.

I yelled for Miss Kolb. I asked, "You must have a name Miss Kolb? What is it? Sue Ellen? Cissie Fran? Gertrude Jean?"

She hooted with delight. "Lord, no. It's Evelyn Linda. Or Evvie Lynn. It makes up my first name, the combination of both. Cute, isn't it?"

"Not as cute as you," I told her. "I was just wondering why women down South use both their names."

She frowned thoughtfully. "I don't really know. I've never even thought about it. What started you off on that?"

My hand gestured at the newspaper lying on the floor. Evvie Lynn bent to pick it up, and her uniform gaped nicely. She had changed brassieres, I saw. She was wearing a black one now. Couple of days ago, it had been a white one.

Her hands smoothed over the paper. She began to read. I listened with half a mind, being more intent on the golden gloss of her nylon stockings where they framed her legs. In her mini-skirted uniform that rode up on her thighs, I got a good look at her excellent underpinnings.

Then she said something that took my mind off her legs. I turned my head to stare at her. "How's that again?"

"What?" she asked blankly.

"What did you just say?"

"I was reading from the paper, about the Yule woman. She's one of the richest people in this part of the country, you know. Her husband made a fortune in textiles, up Greensboro way. She used to be a rodeo star, years back. It say here she was lucky to escape injury when her car

30

motor exploded. I understand she's considering making a comeback on the rodeo circuit. She doesn't have to do it, you understand, she's worth millions. It's just that she's bored, I imagine."

"What Yule woman?" I asked.

"Why, Wanda Weaver Yule. Right here. The——"

"Yaaaa-hoooo!"

I reached out, grabbed her, yanked her over on me and kissed her. "Wanda Weaver Yule, honey! That's the one!"

Evvie Lynn Kolb gulped. "The one what?"

"Make believe you've been knocked out. You're rehearing things through fuzzy eardrums. What does Wanda Weaver Yule sound like?"

"Wander wherever you will?" she asked doubtfully.

So I had slurred the words to make it sound that way, but she got the message. Only she had not heard my tape recorder, so it didn't mean a thing to her.

"A telephone! I need a telephone and the telephone number of that hotel at Manns Harbor where the boss-man is staying."

Five minutes later, Walrus-moustache said he was on his way.

As I replaced the phone, I glanced up at the redhead. She was hovering over me in the downstairs hall where the telephone was as if she expected me to collapse at any moment. Hell, I was fine. My discovery of the murder victim was doing me more good than a shot of insulin for a diabetes patient.

Oooops! I had to censor that tape recording before the boss-man arrived. "Upstairs," I shouted at Miss Kolb. "And hurry!"

I made her close the door again while I worked on the tape recorder. She gave me an arch look as she left. She was no fool, Evvie Lynn.

The tape was nice and proper by the time Walrus-moustache came storming into the bedroom. I made him sit down, I played the tape for him. Then I explained about "wander wherever you will" and how it formed the name of Wanda Weaver Yule.

"Sounds good," he admitted. "But why would anybody

31

want to kill her? As far as I know, she's clean. No bad habits, has no enemies, treats her employees real good. I asked about her at Manns Harbor."

"I don't know why they want to kill her, they just do. Now let me get dressed and I'll go visit her with you. Maybe she knows why."

CHAPTER THREE

Wanda Weaver Yule was an attractive woman in her forties.

She sat in a blue velvet wingback chair with her legs crossed, and let her wide green eyes insult me. Her slim body was encased in a white satin Geno of California pajama dress, strings of beads hung from her neck. The beads were black, her hair was silver, her mouth was a dark red.

"Are you sure?" she was asking in a controlled coloratura voice. "It really doesn't make any sense at all to me."

"I'm quite sure," I replied. "Wanda Weaver Yule, the name was. It came out slurred as 'wander wherever you will.' "

She looked at Walrus-moustache with those green eyes that seemed to tell him I was a mongoloid idiot. The Old Man cleared his throat.

"He is correct, madam. I'll stake my life on it."

"We don't want to stake your life," I said to Mrs. Yule.

She threw up her hands in exasperation. There were half a dozen diamond rings on her fingers. Maybe a hundred thousand dollars worth of diamonds. The sunlight streaming in through the patio door of her living room reflected prismatic rainbows from the jewels.

"That's the most ridiculous thing I've ever heard," she exclaimed, looking around the room. "Two girls want to kill me, you say. You can't tell me why, and I know I certainly cannot tell you. Yet you both believe it."

"We don't want them to kill you," I pointed out.

33

"Otherwise we wouldn't be here. We have only your best interests in mind."

"The item in the newspaper about your accident, when your motor exploded, may have been an attempt on your life. The girls who thought they'd killed me had a try at killing you themselves. It failed, so they'll have another go at it."

"I think you're high on speed," she murmured. She seemed to brighten at the thought. "Are you? I've never dared try speed. Marijuana, yes. I've smoked pot for ages. Love the effect it gives. These modern messiahs of the mind drugs—I think they're so brave, so daring. Columbuses of the chemical cult, I call them. I wish I could be one of the 'inner people' who get down inside their minds and take trips. But I read about the terrible effects these drugs have and I chicken out."

The Chief was staring at her like she'd grown another head. His was a sturdy, sane world, with no place for hippies, yippies or speedsters.

I thought I understood Wanda Weaver Yule. She was hung up on something, she yearned for a lost youth, perhaps, which is why she liked to consider herself a mod, mod doll. The beads, the ultra-sophisticated white satin lounging pajamas, all added up.

She wanted to be an acidhead, she read everything she could get her hands on about smoking grass, about the new STP that sends you on a three or four-day trip instead of the eight to twelve-hour trip of LSD. She believed firmly in the 'turn on, tune in, drop out' philosophy, but she was too innately cautious—or too chicken, as she phrased it—to take chances on ruining her mind and body by indulging in her beliefs.

Maybe I knew what she was hung up on.

I said softly, "Somebody wants to kill you, ma'am."

"Utter nonsense! I have enemies, of course. What rich woman without a husband hasn't? A lot of people around here think I'm a freak, just because I believe in the new social attitudes sweeping the world. Why must there be war? Why can't people love one another?"

"Human nature is———" I began.

34

"—is a catchword, no more!" she flared. "Mankind itself has been reaching for its own Utopia for thousands of years. There used to be slavery, now there is slavery only in the Arab world. Can't you see? Man himself is striving to obey that Christian law, to love his neighbor."

"I couldn't agree with you more," I said. "Love is the universal language. I teach love for your fellow-man in courses at the university where I am a sociology professor. All through Time, man has been struggling to know himself. Maybe one day he will achieve that knowledge. Until then, however, there are a number of people who don't go along with your flowers for fists doctrine. Those are the people we're dealing with right now."

"Well, I certainly don't want to die," she muttered. "I have too much to live for."

Her hand made a swing through the air, to indicate the luxurious furnishings of the room. Wanda Weaver Yule fitted into this background.

I felt out of place; so did Walrus-moustache, because he kept squirming uneasily in a pink armchair. His eyes glared at me, as if to tell me to go on carrying the ball. He was out of his depth with this woman.

She said slowly, "I haven't always had this wealth, you understand. I was a trick rider and roper in the rodeo when my husband saw me and fell in love. He was miles above me in education and culture, but I employed tutors after he married me, to get where I am today." She sighed and her slippered foot swung back and forth.

"I suppose I shall have to permit it," she murmured. "Some sort of personal bodyguard, that is. But it seems ridiculous."

I smiled in my most agreeable way. "We don't want to intrude on your privacy, but we feel someone must be with you at all times, for your protection."

Her thin eyebrows arched again. "At all times?"

"If you'd rather have a Foundation girl—"

"No, no. I wouldn't feel as safe with a girl as I would with you. But what excuse will I give for your presence?"

"I'll be your chauffeur, your butler."

"I have a chauffeur and a butler, but I suppose I could

35

give them a holiday. Oh, what nonsense. Nobody wants to kill me. I just don't believe this fairy tale for one moment."

"But just suppose it isn't a fairy tale. Suppose it were true. You would be in great danger. You are too young, too lovely a woman to throw her life away because the idea of someone trying to kill you seems ridiculous."

Wanda Weaver Yule preened a little for me, smiling for the first time and patting the back of her silver hair with a carefully manicured hand.

I went on. "Surely, you must admit that my superior and myself are not getting anything out of this, except the knowledge of your safety. Why should we go to all of this bother unless we actually believe you are in danger?"

"Very well, you'll be my chauffeur. My butler I insist on retaining. You shall accompany me everywhere. You will even sleep in my bedroom."

Walrus-moustache harrumphed. Wanda Weaver Yule turned to him. "Don't you agree? Should I not be safer that way—with this man right there to protect me?"

This was quite a change coming over our hostess. If she had disliked the idea of her privacy being invaded before, now she was all for it. I wondered what kind of thoughts she was having behind her carefully contrived exterior. Apparently the flint of my words had struck the steel of her opposition and produced a spark somewhere. She was enjoying that spark more than somewhat.

Walrus-moustache got to his feet. "If you don't mind, then, I'll be running along. I'll leave Professor Damon to work out the details."

I went out to the gravel circle fronting the house with him, where he got into his big black limousine, chauffeur-driven. When I went back into the house, she was admiring herself in front of a standing mirror in the hall, twirling her strands of beads and glancing at me over her white satin shoulder, as if to make sure I had a good look at her. She was worth looking at all right. She was slim but she had mature curves. The white satin pajama-dress set them off perfectly.

"Well, now," she said after a while. "I suppose you'll
36

need a uniform. To be my chauffeur, I mean. We have some spares, I think. One of them ought to fit you. Shall we go and see?"

"Yes, ma'am," I said like a chauffeur should.

We walked upstairs, Wanda Weaver Yule first. I could see her buttocks pressing into white satin, moving gently to her walk. I tried not to look but I am only human, and she had a nice behind.

To get my mind off her cheeks, I asked. "Why'd you change your mind back there, Mrs. Yule? You were fighting me for all you were worth, then all of a sudden you got enthusiastic about the idea of my being here with you."

Her laughter woke echoes in the big hall where the winding staircase made a carpeted spiral to the second floor. The Yule home had been a Southern mansion before and during the Civil War. It was as spit-polished today as it had been during the era when slaves had done the work.

I was impressed with this lavish living. I admit it. I might not have fitted into such luxury—hell! I'm only a university professor—but I sure would have enjoyed it. There was a crystal chandelier hanging in the lower hall-way that must have been worth ten thousand dollars, at least.

"I realized who you are," she murmured, stopping on the landing and turning with a ringed hand gripping the mahogany rail. "You are Professor Rod Damon, the founder of the League for Sexual Dynamics, aren't you?"

I had stopped on the stair below her on the landing. My head was level with her head, and her lipsticked mouth was within kissing distance. She had kissing in her eyes too. As a sexpert, I get to know the signs.

"I am. I also work for the Coxe Foundation as a kind of sideline. But why should this knowledge change your mind?"

"Oh, Professor! You ask a silly question, you'll get a silly answer. I know Mary Lou Talbot, who, shall we say, studied under you."

"Ah," I nodded, remembering Mary Lou Talbot as a bit of delicious Southern-fried chick who really dug my

L.S.D. lectures. I asked thoughtfully, "And this makes a difference?"

She beamed on me with her kissable lips; she laughed at me with her green eyes; I guess she had me tabbed for a schnook. A stupid schnook, at that. She leaned closer and whispered, "I've been a widow for seven years, Professor. I thought having you around might cure my loneliness."

"As well as save your life," I nodded, still playing it stupid, trying to ignore the way her white satin pajama blouse clung to her breasts. The breasts were full and heavy, judging by their outlines.

She put a fingertip on my lips and traced them. Her eyes were green fires. She nodded, and her tonguetip came out to run about her lips. "Maybe you can teach me why I want to stay alive."

"I'm sure I can," I nodded.

There are times when my dual personality as founder of L.S.D. and as a Coxeman overlap. This was to be one of them. By means of my sex expertise, I might improve my secret service image.

I did not hurry things. I simply put a palm on her leg behind the knee and ran it up to her pouting buttock. Under the white satin her flesh felt smooth, well-cared-for. She shivered and her mouth fell open.

"Here?" she breathed.

My hand patted her behind, making the cheeks jiggle. "Certainly not. We're going to look at uniforms."

I turned her around and gave her backside a little push. She half-laughed, ruefully, and said, "I thought you were a real expert, Professor. Is this how you do your thing?"

"The first rule of loving is never to rush," I admonished her gently, trailing her up the stairs to the second floor. "Take your time, enjoy it. You'll discover I mean what I say—a little later on."

She glanced at me archly over her shoulder, sighing, "If you say so. But I must admit to a sense of disappointment."

"Tell me that before you fall asleep," I chided her.

The room with the spare uniforms was at the end of the hall. It held maids' uniforms, chauffeurs' uniforms, mops

38

and pails and dust rags. Spare drapes, extra bedcovers, curtains and shades, were piled in here as neatly as possible.

She lifted a coat, held it out to me. It was of blue serge. Pale blue trousers went with it. I slipped the coat on while Wanda Yule held the trousers over an arm. The jacket fitted to perfection.

"Now the pants," she nodded.

I removed the jacket, then unbuckled my belt, casting an inquiring look at my employer. She smiled blandly back at me.

"I've seen men in their shorts before," she said.

So I shrugged and pushed my pants down, showing my lean middle and the more or less tight jockey shorts. She put her eyes to the reinforced cup and her tongue came out to lick her lips. There was a yearning in her green eyes that I recognized as the call of the wanting widow.

My manhood was responding by automatic reflex to the heat in her stare. I had to get those trousers on before I got embarrassed. She was having none of it. She pulled the pants away with a jerk of her ringed hands.

"Wait," she breathed. "You're built like a stallion."

"But this is no place for horseplay."

"I know, I know," she sighed. "Just let me look."

So she looked and longed and when I responded as she knew I would, from what Mary Lou Talbot had told her, her hands began shaking. But she was a lady, or she thought she was; at the moment, there might have been some doubt about that, and about her role in life as a culture vulture. All she knew for certain was that she was ready, willing and able to have a roll in the hay with me.

Her hands cupped the pouch of my briefs lovingly.

"Later," I reminded her, thrusting her hands away.

She sighed and handed over the trousers. They fit reasonably well, they were slightly baggy at the waist, so she said I'd have to go to the tailor and have them fitted properly.

"I'd better go now, then," I said.

"But hurry back. It's a warm day and I want to go for a swim in the pool." Her lips smiled, her eyes filled with gleeful hunger. "You'll want to take a swim with me too, to prevent anybody from killing me, so you'd better get yourself a pair of swim trunks."

I would do that, I promised.

She let me borrow a gold Shelby Cobra GT 500-KR which she used to race around the country roads. It was a beautiful machine. Driving it, I really did feel like a king of the road, as the Ford people say in their advertisements.

I braked before a complex of Tudor buildings which was the local shopping center. There was a department store, a hobby crafts shop, a boutique where the girls bought their glamour goodies, a stationery store, a tailor shop, a laundry, a jewelry store.

I went to visit the tailor.

While he was measuring me, the little man with the goatee and the balding head informed me that Wanda Weaver Yule was an angel. It was her money that had given him and the jeweler and the man who owned the laundromat the chance to make a go of things in the shopping compound.

"Ah never saw her like," he murmured, rubbing the wax marker along the back of the pants. "Charges three puhcent int'rest. Never presses for it, neither."

"Makes loans, does she?" I asked, not at all curious, but anxious to have him go on talking.

"To little people, to big people, to anybody who needs cash. She's an angel, an uttuh angel. Helps everybody."

I wondered if somebody she had loaned money to was anxious to write her off as a creditor. I asked, "Anyone around here owe her so much money he might kill her?"

The man was shocked. "Kill Missus Yule? Never!"

Maybe not. Maybe so. "How are you doing financially?"

"Never better. I'm fixin' to buy a house, 'stead of the apartment where my missus and I live."

"Glad to hear it."

"Ah never charge her for my services. It's a mattuh of pride with me. These pants, foh example. Ah'll have them for you tonight, you wan 'em that fast. Be a pleasure too."

40

"Tomorrow will do," I grinned.

I drove back to Heather Haven, the name of the Yule estate, in a very thoughtful mood. Could be one of her generosities was backfiring on Wanda Weaver Yule. However, this made little sense. Nobody who owed her money would have enough capital to go around hiring girls to employ professional assassins. If a debtor had that much cash on hand, he could pay back what he owed.

Or would he? I decided to ask Wanda about it.

She was at poolside as I parked the car in the graveled drive, yoohooing at me and waving a tanned arm. I came around the side of a brick retaining wall to see a sloping lawn leading down onto a flat stretch of grass in which a kidney-shaped pool was set. The water in the pool was a pale blue that made the whole thing resemble a giant sapphire surrounded by the white satin of the poolside tiling and the green velvet of the neatly clipped lawn.

"I'm already out," she caroled, getting to her feet.

She was wearing a skimpy black bikini, the bottom section of which just about covered her front and bared more than half her behind, while the upper part consisted of two tiny cups supporting the somewhat heavy breasts nestling and jiggling inside them.

She saw the package in my hands. "You bought a swimsuit? Good! Go put it on—oh, not inside. There, by the hydrangea bush—there's a sort of trellis."

The trellis would hide me from the house, it would not shield me from Wanda Weaver Yule. I looked from the trellis to her almost naked body, and chuckled. "So much for your voyeuristic tendencies."

I slid out of my clothes while my hostess lighted a cigarette and stood beside the pool staring at my nakedness. Since she was so interested, I didn't bother to turn my back. If she wanted a private sneak peek, let her look. She stared, forgetting to puff on her cigarette. I tried to cram myself into the swim trunks I'd bought back at the shopping center. They were no more than a posing strap. It was a tough job, and the green eyes admiring my king-sized manhood didn't help.

Of course the suit hid very little so I ran down the

grassy slope and out onto the diving board. The board gave under my weight as I took off in a high jack-knife. The water came up to swallow me but not before I heard Mrs. Yule applauding my performance.

I went through the water like a dolphin. To one side of me there was a flash of flesh and black bikini, and my employer bumped into me as I rose to the surface. My arms went about her to prevent her from getting hurt, but she misunderstood my gesture.

"Mmmmm," she hummed, rubbing against me, locking her wet arms about my neck. "This is the life."

It was indeed. She was a needing female and I had been on a starvation diet since that afternoon with Laura Ogden and Midge Priest. I let my palms slip down her naked back to her curving hips, outward across them to the buttocks covered only by the thin spaghetti straps of her bikini bottom. My fingers tightened in the soft flesh.

She moaned, grinding her pelvis onto my own bulging loins. Back and forth she worked her hips, scrunching lower, fastening her legs around mine for purchase. Her panting filled the air.

After a moment, during which her fleshy body shook uncontrollably, she whispered, "Not here either, I suppose?"

"Certainly not," I laughed, holding her close.

She bit my shoulder gently, then licked it with her tongue. "If anybody were to try and kill me now, I almost wouldn't mind."

"Go ahead. Remind me I'm not doing my duty."

"But you are, you are," she protested, tightening the grip of her arms about my neck. "You're doing fine."

"Just the same, I have a few questions to ask you."

"Must you?" she pleaded, pressing into me.

I drew her with me toward the pool rim. I turned and hoisted her up onto the edge, her buttocks slapping the stone edge wetly as she landed. A moment later, I was there beside her.

"The tailor tells me you're an angel," I began. "You lend money to everybody. He says there isn't anything a hundred people wouldn't do for you."

42

"I have money, they don't. I try to equalize things." She pouted as an afterthought, "But you don't. You're mean. You know what I want and I have what you want, but we aren't sharing our wealth."

"We shall," I promised, "after you tell me all the people you've loaned money to."

Her eyebrows arched. "You don't really expect me to remember them all, do you? I'm not much of a businesswoman when it comes to things like that. About the factories and the stores I own—yes. There I keep a staff of accountants and lawyers to protect my interests, but as for my personal loans, as I consider them, I don't pay much attention to details."

"You must have some records!"

"None, Professor. Almost absolutely none. It is a personal thing with me, those loans. I give ten thousand dollars here, a hundred thousand there. Even a million or two, at times."

"A m-million? And you have no records?"

One tanned shoulder lifted casually. "It is my hobby. Oh, I guess I do remember a few people, here and there. A professor of literature, to write a book. A doctor of physics, to finish an invention. A young man with a good business background, to start his own firm. That sort of thing."

We would have to make an inventory, I told her. We would write out a list of her debtors and the amounts they owed her, as best she could remember them. I was quite determined about it. It was the only clue we might have as to her would-be murderer.

Wanda was almost shocked at the idea.

"None of them would every kill me, not for money! I know it. I refuse to even consider the idea. No, no. I won't be talked into it. Come! Let's go back into the pool!"

When she finally pulled herself out, it was growing dusk. We were to eat dinner in the dining room at eight o'clock. I had a while to shave and get dressed. She was going to wear an evening gown, but I could make do with the business suit that was draped over a hydrangea bush.

In my room, I lay down on the bed and thought.

43

The realization dawned on me that I was no nearer the solution of this case than I had been when I'd been surf-casting along the Outer Banks. Sure, I knew two girls were involved in a plot to kill Wanda Weaver Yule. At least, I thought I did.

But, "Wander wherever you will" might not mean Wanda Weaver Yule at all. And in that case, I was on a fool's errand here in this Southern mansion. One thing I did know. Laura Ogden and Midge Priest were involved in the plot. They had damn near killed me, and they wanted to murder somebody else.

I was dozing a little on the bed when Molly woke me by knocking on the door. It was twenty to eight, she informed me, and the mistress was expecting me in the library-den for cocktails. I thanked her and got dressed.

I made a reasonably presentable appearance, I imagine, as I joined my hostess at the bar in the library-den. Her green eyes actually glowed at sight of me.

"Manhattans? Martinis?" she asked gaily.

My eyes ran over the bottle-laden glass shelves behind the mahogany bar. "Let me," I replied. "Let me make the drinks. I have a B.B.A. degree, you know—Best Bartender Anywhere."

She giggled but relaxed on one of the high stools in front of the bar, and waved a diamond-braceleted arm at the bottles. "Indulge yourself, Best Bartender."

Wanda was poured into a gold lamé evening gown. Its middle hugged her slim waist and curving hips, its bodice barely contained her breasts. Its mini-skirt showed off her bewitching legs in liquid-look stockings.

She put her elbows on the bar and stared as I built a Montgomery—named after the field marshal—a martini made fifteen parts gin to one of vermouth.

My hostess sipped. "Ooooh—it's delicious!" she exclaimed.

"Just one more of my many talents," I grinned.

We savored our Montgomerys while we talked about the national drinks of many countries. When I expressed surprise at the completeness of her bar, Wanda Weaver Yule confessed that her husband, while not a compulsive

44

drinker, enjoyed experimenting with liquors.

"He'd lose himself back there behind the bar," she said. "He'd see a new recipe for a drink and nothing would satisfy him until he made it. He didn't like all those he made, but he had a favorite few. He liked to say each liquor was different, that some blended with some, others were individuals."

"I feel that way about people."

"Some people respond to kind treatment, others need a whip hand. I use the whip hand in business, but as far as individuals go, I like to play at—yes, at good angel, I guess. Fairy godmother. I give people their tangible dreams. I'm like a *deus ex machina*."

"How about me? Would you stake me if I asked?"

"At what?"

"I could open a sex education school."

Her head moved back and forth. "Not you. You aren't keen enough on your own idea. You have it made now. You're a university professor, you're the founder of that League for Sexual Dynamics. You don't really want to open any school."

"I take it personal enthusiasm makes a big difference?"

"Naturally! A man won't make a success at something he isn't enthusiastic about. And he won't be about something he doesn't love. You give me enthusiasm and love, and that's a pretty powerful combination. It spells success. If all a man needs is money—I give it to him."

I leaned over the bar and kissed her cheek.

She actually flushed.

"Damn you! I mean it," she protested.

"I'm admiring you," I told her with enthusiasm. "It makes me want to cuddle and protect you even more."

"Mmmm, I'd like that," she said, smiling lazily. "I'd like it even more if you did your thing with me instead of putting it off and sublimating your sex drive with words and promises."

"I've been building you up and then letting you down, haven't I? All talk and no play makes Rod Damon a very dull fellow, I'm afraid."

45

"We-eell," she drawled, her eyes gleeful as I came around the bar.

As I stood behind her, my lips ran across her bare shoulder up to her soft throat. From this perspective I could feast my eyeballs on the soft bulges of her breasts trapped inside the gold lamé bodice of her evening gown. I was about to make myself indespensable to this rich society woman.

"Care to let me handle dinner?" I murmured.

She shivered voluptuously. "Any time," she murmured throatily.

"Then we'll eat in your room—my way."

"The table's all set," she whispered.

My lips were on her earlobe, drawing that perfumed tidbit of female flesh between them, my teeth nibbling gently. I whispered, "I'll carry the trays and dishes upstairs to your bedroom."

Her green-tinted eyelids flickered. She was beginning to catch on. The plump white mounds in her bodice lifted and shook more rapidly.

"What should I do?" she asked.

"Give the servants a night off. Or make sure they don't come up into the bedroom. They might be a little—shocked, shall I say?—at our eating habits."

We went into the huge kitchen that flanked the dining room. The cook and a pretty maid goggled at me as I took a big silver tray from the dining room, piled on the platters of oysters Rockeller and the *coq au vin* and marched out with Wanda Weaver Yule at my heels, carrying plates and knives and forks, spoons, cups and glasses on a serving tray.

"Maddy, bring the wine—two bottles," she was saying. "After that both of you can have the night off." Her voice broke twice as she spoke, I rather imagine she was wondering just how we were going to eat this epicurean feast.

Her bedroom was something out of a movie spectacular. It was half of the entire upper floor. At one end was her king-size four-poster bed, the valance and bed coverlet done in royal blue satin. The bed was flanked on one wall by a fireplace with a bronze hood, with easy

46

chairs on either side. There was a picture window across from the fireplace; its heavy, pale blue drapes were pulled shut. A thick blue rug was spread across the parqueted floor.

The other end of the room held an oak secretary with a chair before it, so that when the writing board was pulled down, one could use it as a desk. Two straightbacked chairs were on either side of the secretary, just below twin windows. Another picture window was to the left of the secretary. It matched its duplicate, and was as heavily pull-draped.

In the middle of the room was a chaise lounge. Between the picture windows was a dressing table with an absolutely gigantic mirror. Its bench was covered with ocelot fur that matched the sides of the table itself.

This was the formal Wanda Weaver Yule.

Along two long walls, the secret Wanda Weaver Yule was visible. There were posters of all sizes and descriptions hung for her to see when she wanted to brood on her new society. Psychedelic art paintings and photographs were grouped about a light organ which would throw colored lights around the room when turned on. A stereo phonograph could blare out the musical media of the mod world when she was in the mood.

A satiric assemblage by Marisol stood cheek by jowl beside a boxed imagery by Cornell. On the walls, where the posters yielded room, I made out a black stripe painting by Stella, a bit of pop art by Oldenburg, a lifesize plaster mannikin by Segal.

It was somewhat overwhelming, but I told myself to ignore the surroundings and concentrate on my mission for the moment. At one time, this room must have been two; a wall had been knocked down to make it into an enormous bedchamber. Now the room was something more than just a place to sleep. It was a mirror for the woman deep inside Wanda Weaver Yule. I noticed there were no rodeo trappings anywhere in the room. Was she ashamed of her former heritage? But no matter. I gathered that Wanda Weaver Yule could live very comfortably in here.

47

If she wanted to be business-like, the secretary would accommodate her. I told myself there might be secrets in that piece of furniture. It might repay me as a Coxeman to know about that. Later, after we had used the king-sized bed or maybe the chaise lounge for our embraces, I would have a look at that secretary.

When I had set up our feast on the night tables, which I placed in the middle of the spacious bedroom. I turned to the still goggling maid, who was clutching two wine bottles to her bosom. "You run along, Maddy. The mistress and I are going to indulge in a special kind of dietary dinner. It's my own invention, and I don't want anybody to know the secret."

Maddy was actually squirming with curiosity, but after I took the wine bottles and slid them into twin ice buckets, I took her elbow and guided her toward the thick oaken bedroom door. I escorted her out into the hall, then closed and bolted the door. Wanda Weaver Yule was just as curious as her servant girl. Her green eyes were big with wonder.

"Is this really a dietary dinner?"

"It is. I omitted one very important word from my description to Maddy. In essence, this is a dietary diddle-thon."

The green eyelids blinked. She made a beautiful picture in the gold lamé, with her diamond rings and bracelets, with the diamond necklace on her upper chest. Her face was a perfect blend of healthy flesh and the finest makeup money can buy. There was gold dust on her eyelashes as well as that green stuff on her eyelids. Her lips were a brilliant scarlet, her silver hair was coiffed in an upsweep, with a diamond pin set in the center of a swirled strand.

I stood admiring her for long moments.

"You look good enough to eat," I told her softly, advancing across the thick Wilton carpet. "And eat you I shall. But first we must be presentable for this special type of dining."

I went behind her, sought and found the zipper of her gown. I drew it down and sowed kisses along her backbone as the zipper descended. She gave a muted little

48

cry, and then was silent. The tab went down to the cleavage line of her buttocks, some inches below the red lace and lastex band of a garterbelt.

My lips touched her sacral dimples set just above each buttock. After a time she gasped, "Please! Please!" Her body was shaking like an aspen in a gale. She smelled all over of perfume, and her skin was warm cream under my mouth.

She wore nothing but the garterbelt and sheer nylons under the gold lamé. I pushed aside the gold lamé with my head as my mouth pastured across a bare hip and up above the red garterbelt strap to her naked side.

"I c-can't take it a-any more," she sobbed.

My teeth nipped her soft flesh, then I walked around in front of her and reached for the oysters Rockefeller. I took one on an oyster fork and raised it to her open mouth. She was not reaching for the oyster with those parted scarlet lips, she was just trying to breathe.

"Who—who wants food?" she wailed.

I put the oyster fork down. I began undressing.

Her green eyes were wide as they watched me. When I stood like Priapus come alive before her, she cried, "Oh my God! Stop torturing me!"

"If you don't want oysters Rockefeller, I do, darling," I whispered.

My hands went to the gold lamé gown. I drew it away from her breasts slowly. She closed her eyes and made throaty sounds as her breasts sprang out into the light. They were big, heavy, very white with blue veins just beneath the surface. Her nipples were huge, thickly swollen.

With the sauce bucket, I coated her nipples liberally with the lemon sauce usually served with this dish. I forked a mouthful of the oysters Rockefeller and then used the lemon sauce on her nipples to flavor it. I munched each nipple with my every chew, until her hands came up and caught my head.

"You devil! Oh, God—you wonderful devil," she breathed.

She was writhing her thighs together and swinging her hips like a hula dancer in her erotic excitement. Her eyes

49

blazed with understanding and delight. Now she became a partner in our dietary delights.

As I had done to her, so she did to me, using her sharp white teeth to bite into my tiny nubs. She still wore the lower half of her evening gown; she was a topless diner, instead of a topless waitress.

Her cheeks were flushed, her eyes sparkled.

When the oysters were gone, after we alternated with the application of the lemon sauces between her nipples and mine, I reached for a wine bottle chilling in an ice bucket. I popped the cork and poured.

"To our dinner," I proposed.

"And most of all—the main dish," she giggled.

"For that, you're overdressed," I grinned.

I knelt before her. My hands went to the gold lamé bunched about her white hips. I drew the material down, kissing her soft white belly as I bared it. She moaned and whimpered, deep in the throes of an erotic frenzy.

When the gown was pooled about her slippered feet, I drew back to admire her body. She kept herself in good trim, her legs were shapely, strongly curved at calf and thigh; in the black nylons and red garterbelt, she was a centerfold come to life. Her flesh was tanned except for the white bowls of her breasts and the tiny triangle where her Venus fur grew.

I reached for the *coq au vin*.

With a chicken breast drenched in wine sauce, I smeared her upper thighs. Then I took a bite of the *coq* and lapped off the Burgundy sauce. She was a blend of wine sauce and perfumed womanhood, she was absolutely delicious both to my tongue and to my nostrils.

The chicken tasted pretty good, too.

Then it was her turn and she tantalized me until I yelled as a safety valve for my emotions. She was not content with my thighs, she put the sauce where I did my thing. And she took her time about eating, sitting on a footstool before me, taking little nibbles of the chicken and big licks of the sauce.

"I won't do any more eating," she giggled. "I don't want to waste your strength."

50

"You can't," I told her.

She stared up at me, plucked eyebrows wrinkled.

I explained, "I'm afflicted with priapism, honey. The ability to maintain my arousal indefinitely. No matter how hard I try—or you try, for that matter—my maleness cannot be exhausted."

She arched her right eyebrow, showing me her disbelief.

"Fact," I told her eyebrow. "Try it and see."

"Oh no. I like you as you are. Rearing to go."

I grinned. "Nobody ever believes me. I always have to prove what I say. Okay, then. I'll prove it. Have you ever heard of Philaenis of Samos? Samos is an island in the Aegean Sea. Philaenis is a woman who lived there once, devoting much of her time to making love and then writing about it."

Wanda shook her silver head. "I don't know the lady."

"Aeschrion mentions her, so does Suetonius and Lucian. Unfortunately, much of her work is lost. The Roman emperor Tiberius commissioned artists to illustrate her writings in paintings and sculptures with which he adorned his sleeping quarters."

"How many positions?" my hostess asked.

"Nobody knows. From the few fragments I've been lucky enough to lay hands on in my trips to Europe, I'd judge at least sixty."

"Sixty!"

"Oh, most of them are only variations of the basic ones. It's always been my ambition to try out Philaenis in the flesh. I have yet to find a woman who can go beyond the first twelve."

Her red tongue ran around her lipsticked mouth. "Try me," she whispered, putting her palms on my rockhard thighs and sliding them upward.

"All right," I agreed. "We'll begin with the preliminaries."

I caught her head and drew her face toward me.

Ten minutes later, I brought her to her bed, and stretched her out on her back so that her legs dangled over the edge. I knelt down and feasted on her flesh until she was screaming thickly.

51

It was then that I resorted to Philaenis. . . .

Four and a half hours later, my hostess was unconscious.

I lay on the rumpled bed with her, my head pillowed on its twisted covers. Our bodies were still in a variant of the *Venus reversa* position. Wanda Weaver Yule lay face down, her torso between my parted feet, her thighs resting on my hips. She was snoring slightly.

I had read her correctly, all right. She was hung up on the new society, on the need to make love, not war, because she herself was desperate for sexual attention. It was Wanda Weaver Yule who wanted to make love, who thought and preached that doctrine when she could.

She would scream, "Ride 'em, cowboy!" as she flopped helplessly in her orgasmic spasm. From time to time her voice would cry out, "Make love! Make love!"

I was a bit winded after four and a half hours.

She slept peacefully, dead to our world. It was easy to slide out from under the weights of her thighs, to arrange her more comfortably amid the bedcovers, to throw a blanket over her nudity.

Then I turned my attention to her secretary. A simple tug told me it was locked. I went to her dressing table, selected a hairpin and returned to the secretary. Inserting the hairpin, I worked it around until the drawer lock clicked open.

At the end of half an hour, I was positive the secretary was no help to me. I had hoped, despite the fact that I enjoyed being both bodyguard and lover to this woman, that I would find some paper, some document, in these drawers that would pinpoint a possible murderer and his motive for wanting to kill Wanda Weaver Yule. If I learned a name, I could strike at the would-be killer without waiting for him or her to strike first.

As it was, Wanda Weaver Yule had to be the bait for her own killer. I had to stay here and prevent her murder—and it had occurred to me that I might fail.

CHAPTER FOUR

Wanda Weaver Yule was madder than a wet cat.

She stood in her bedroom wearing a pair of green nylon panties and high-heeled shoes, cursing me up and down. Her hand had hold of a crystal atomizer. With an anguished howl and a sweep of her bare right arm, she flung it at me.

It grazed my temple as I ducked.

"Look, honey," I said, "it's only for a few hours!"

"I will not! I will not go to that mod ball with anybody but you," she screeched. Her big white breasts wobbled crazily as she made motions with her hands. "That old fogey you call Walrus-moustache is not, I repeat, is not going to be my dancing partner all night long!"

"But I'm on duty! It's my job to protect you!"

She muttered something I cannot repeat. Regally, she crossed her arms about her jumping mammaries and looked down her nose at me. She was one angry female, flushed and almost weeping. I had to do something to calm her down, to put sense in her shapely skull.

I walked across the room, slid my arms about her, and kissed her. She was warm and soft and cuddly when I was through.

"You see?" she purred with female logic. "You see how well we get on together? And you want me to go to the ball with somebody else."

"All he's going to do is dance with you."

"No!"

I kissed her soft neck with searching lips and darting tongue. She giggled and rubbed her thighs against me. She

53

was an exciting woman. She excited me and she knew it. My head bent so I could let my mouth pasture on her right breast. Wanda panted a little and rubbed her soft white thighs together.

"Mmmmm. It's still no," she whispered.

She was not as positive, however. I touched her stiffened brown nipples with my tonguetip. She began panting and shoving her belly against me.

"I'll drive you there and guard you," I told her big white breasts with my kissing lips. "I'll take Walrus-moustache home and then you and I will be together for the whole time."

Apparently she thought that over, because she asked in a weak voice, "Do you really think I'm in danger?"

"I do. If you get killed, we wouldn't be able to have a party later, after the ball. I want you alive and healthy, you delicious thing."

She thawed and pushed away from me. "All right, all right. I'll go with your old Walrus-moustache."

"You might even like him, you know. He isn't at all bad-looking," I reassured her. "And I understand he's a real good dancer."

She shrugged casually, a wicked glint in her green eyes. "Call your silly Walrus-moustache, then. But you've got to help me bathe and dress." When I opened my mouth to protest, she murmured innocently, "If I'm in all that much danger, I don't want you to leave my side for a single moment."

I nodded, giving her pouting lips a final kiss before I moved for the telephone. While I was dialing, my hostess began humming and walking about the room, waiting until I was dialing before she paused, bending over to slide her green nylon panties down off her fleshy hips. I found myself staring at a pair of plump buttocks just as Walrus-moustache spoke.

"Hello?"

"Chief, this is Damon. I'm going to need you to escort Mrs. Yule to that mod ball tonight."

"What, me dance?"

Wanda was undoing my shirt buttons, smiling wickedly.

54

She was going to make me suffer for not forgetting duty long enough to act as her escort.

"Right, I knew you'd go for the idea!"

Angry growls at the other end of the line. Then: "You've been playing nurse to that woman for four days. Hasn't anybody made a try at killing her yet?"

"No, indeed. She—ah—even insists that you take her!"

She bit me just below my belt buckle when I said that, kneeling there and sliding down my uniform pants and jockey shorts.

"This is one of those masquerade things, isn't it? I'll have to wear some stupid costume. You sure you can't protect her and go as her partner?"

"I knew you'd jump at the chance, Chief—ohh!"

Wanda Weaver Yule was playing king-at-arms with me, still kneeling and beginning to coo over a certain effect her feathery fingertips were inducing. She had me as naked as herself, by this time, except for my socks and shoes.

"What's the matter there?"

"Nothing you'd be interested in, Chief. We'll pick you up at nine. By the way, how are you dressing?"

"As a pirate, curse you! And when I see you I'm going to tattoo the Jolly Rodger all over your ugly face!"

His phone slammed down. Wanda sat back on her heels and gazed at me in utter adoration.

I pretended annoyance. "Now look what you've done. We have no time for games. We're due at Walrusmoustache's in about an hour and a half. Scarcely time for you to get bathed and dressed."

She pushed her head against my thigh, giggling fit to bust a gut. "I just wanted to be s-sure your gun was cocked."

I grinned, bending to put hands under her armpits, to lift her. "All right, a quickie then. Come along."

To my surprise, she pulled away. "Oh, no. We have no time for games. That"—and she pointed an accusing finger—"just serves you right for being such a stinker! We are going to bathe me, without any shenanigans."

Her buttocks twitched and dimpled as she strode purposefully toward the bathroom door. I went after them, sighing to myself. I was starting to suffer, in a way. While I am afflicted with priapism, I like to assuage my condition when the opportunity offers. Not to do so for any prolonged period of time makes me hurt.

I hurt while I ran her bath and she crowded her nakedness in against mine, sliding her hands where they would make me suffer most. I helped her into the tub, I soaped a washcloth and while she lay back, I ran it over her wet flesh. Everywhere, while my forehead got moist, and not just from the humidity in the steamy bathroom, I slid it all around her curves.

"I'm beginning to enjoy this sybaritic life," she informed me as my hand with the washcloth cleansed her soapy breasts. "Having a handsome mannish male wait on me is my idea of living it up."

"Living it up is the right term," I muttered.

She smiled at me and ran a wet fingertip along my thigh. "It is, at that," she agreed. "I ought to bathe you too, dear Rod—but we just haven't the time."

My hand steadied her as she stepped from the tub. I ran a big towel over her damp nudity until it was dry. Then there was a big fluffy powderpuff that anointed her flesh with scented whiteness, after which I rubbed her down again.

She had no mercy on me. I must wait on her stark naked, bring her the net stockings, the big white cottontail—she was dressing as a Playboy bunny—the rabbit ears and the blue satin bunny outfit into which she could just about squeeze her mature body.

The effect was sensational. Her shapely legs were on view all the way up to where her plump buttocks oozed more than halfway out of the seat of the tight garment. Her bare shoulders and the way her breasts were pushed upward and outward like squeezed white balloons, would make any man exhibit his badge of manliness.

"You like?" she wondered, turning before a mirror.

"It's time for me to get dressed," I snarled.

I got dressed as fast as I could, looking away from that tantalizing body. I cursed the Coxe Foundation that had put me in such a situation. I cursed Walrus-moustache,

56

who was going to hold this bundle of libidinous flesh in his arms all night. I cursed my unruly priapism.

My hands found an ermine wrap half an hour later. I flung it about her shoulders and ran ahead of her to start the car. We were using the Cadillac tonight. I would be up front behind the wheel, she and the chief would be cuddling behind my back.

I drove as if the hammers of hell were pounding on me. My mood was belligerent and I had the proverbial chip on my shoulder. In short, I was spoiling for a fight.

Walrus-moustache, damn his eyes, was in a jolly mood. As he stepped into the car, he caught Wanda by the hand and pressed his lips to its scented back. I growled in my throat.

"My dear Mrs. Yule, you are perfection," he murmured.

I had all I could do not to boot him one. He looked good in his pirate outfit. He was a regular Edward Teach—Blackbeard—even to the firecrackers tied in the huge mop of black whiskers that half hid his face.

Wanda added to my annoyance by cooing and gurgling like a baby in her delight over his appearance. "You make my heart go all pitter-patter," she informed him in a disgustingly sugary voice. "Here—feel."

That was when I slid behind the wheel.

I was still suffering from my proximity to Wanda Weaver Yule somewhat earlier. I snarled at the Chief, I glared at Wanda, I was practically foaming at the mouth. Mrs. Yule knew it. She smiled sweetly and tapped my cheek with her perfumed fingertips.

"Keep a close watch, Rod," she murmured. "Protect me!"

Walrus-moustache put an arm about her ermine-wrapped pulchritude and strode off into the brightly lighted hotel lobby, leaving me out in the driveway with only the Cadillac to console me. The Cadillac was no consolation.

I ignored the men and women shoving and poking me as they fought to get a closer look. I had to ignore them, or else I would have poked any one of half a dozen clods

57

who stepped on my toes, banged me with their shoulders, pushed me aside, in their desire to look at the rich folk having fun.

I reached my peak of patience when a big hand came down on my shoulder, squeezed tight, and pushed hard. That did it. I turned, saw two big goons marching through the country club lobby the way Sherman had marched through Georgia. I saw red anger, white hate, and blue blazes. I snarled low in my throat. I started after the hoodlums who thought they were so tough.

They were big boys, with wide, muscular shoulders and thick necks. They looked as if they knew how to handle themselves in a fight. I refused to pick on anybody my own size; I wanted somebody even bigger, like those bums going up the staircase. Two of them would be about right, the way I felt. I wanted to relieve my frustrations. A good knock-down-drag-out fight would do the trick. I forgot all about protecting Wanda Weaver Yule.

I walked after them up the big marble staircase with its deeply piled scarlet coverings, and along a corridor until I was standing before the French windows through which my quarry had walked. I opened the French window and stepped out onto the balcony that ran the length of the clubhouse.

I glanced at the driveway. There was nobody down there but the empty cars. Everybody else, including the chauffeurs like me, were standing around the hotel lobby, staring at the party-goers in their costumes. Still, the balcony was a little public to stage the donnybrook I had in mind.

It was quiet here. Out of the corners of my eyes, as I brought out a cigarette, I saw the two big men moving along the balcony. The rhythms of the two orchestras hired for the mod party were faint and seemingly far away. I moved along the narrow balcony which ran completely about the country clubhouse, until I was at the corner of the grand ballroom.

The two men were standing there, peering in through the high windows between the balcony and the ballroom.

One of the men held a naked revolver fitted with a

58

silencer. My blood pulsed like bubbling lava. All the frustrations of the night had me up tight. I should have reached for the revolver in the shoulder holster under my uniform jacket. Instead I ran forward, shouting.

The man with the revolver whirled toward me. His eyes got big as his hand steadied the gun. His companion was peering over his shoulder, shouting hoarsely. "Don't shoot, Lennie! Just zap him one with the barrel."

He was out to earn his murder money. A gunshot might alarm the guests. Zap me and Lennie would have time to take dead aim at Wanda Weaver Yule and fire.

I dived in a flying tackle.

My shoulder hit Lennie across his right thigh, drove him backwards into his companion. The gun whistled as it slashed through the air an inch from my skull. All three of us hit the balcony floor at the same time. I closed my fingers around the Colt .38 and yanked, twisting the gun at the same time.

Lennie screamed. His finger was caught in the trigger guard and the snap I heard was the finger breaking. I sympathized with him only until I had the gun free of his smarting hand. Then I drove the metallic weight of the blue steel revolver full into the side of his jaw.

The man with Lennie was bringing his fist up from the floor. Hard knuckles rammed into my left cheekbone. The stars came down from the sky and danced around my eyes for a few moments.

I leaped through the circling stars at the man with the sideburns. He was off balance after that uppercut he'd popped me with, so I had the right side of his face all to my left fist. My left fist slammed home and he fell sideways into the building wall.

Lennie was erupting into action below me as I was going over him. His fist came up into my middle, knocking some of the wind out of me. I half turned as I bounced off his companion and drove the gun I still held in my hand at his face.

I never connected. The sideburned slugger wrapped me with his flailing arm as he came away from the building wall. That big bar of living flesh drove me into the ornate marble railing. I hung there a moment, trying to get my breath back, cursing the red rage with which I had attacked these two. If I'd drawn my own gun from its shoulder holster and fired when I saw that these two were doing, I wouldn't be in this bag.

Four hands grabbed me, heaving me up, and the railing went away below me. I realized they were going to heave me over the balcony rail to the hard driveway below.

One of my waving hands tangled in thick hair. I tightened my fingers. Somebody began yowling. My other hand flailed around, found more hair. With both hands yanking so hard their scalps were lifted clear of their skulls, I swore that if I went over, these two manhandlers would go with me, or I would pull their scalps off. Both men were screeching in pain below me.

I kicked my legs, I hit Sideburns with a knee right on his nose. Lennie caught a heel in his mouth.

They staggered; their arms got a little weak and my struggling body started coming down to their head-level. I guess they were realizing that we were bringing curious onlookers out of the hotel lobby. I think they wanted out fast, because they took away their hands so my body started to fall. The only trouble with their plan was me. I would not let go of their longish hair.

As my two hundred pounds dropped, my fists moved forward. Since my fists held all that hair between their fingers, their heads went forward—into the hard marble railing. There were a couple of scrunchy sounds.

My weight landed on my toes, behind these hoods who were bending forward with their foreheads slammed into the cold marble, like pilgrims bowing to Mecca. I grated between my teeth, "Now, damn your silly eyes, here's where I get rid of my emotions!"

Bonka bonka bonka.

When I let them go, they sagged.

I stood above their unconscious bodies and drew a few deep breaths. I felt like Tarzan after a battle with a bull gorilla. I wanted to lift my face to the stars and howl.

Half a dozen people had congregated below the balcony, staring up with popping eyes, their jaws open. I waved a hand down at them.

"Can somebody go call a policeman?" I asked.

"No need to do that," a big husky bruiser behind me said. "I'm a state trooper. I'll take over. What's this all about?"

I said, "I found these creeps looking in a window at the ballroom. One of them had a revolver in a hand. It's fitted with a silencer."

I handed the gun to him.

"Okay," he nodded. "Let's go."

Walrus-moustache and a mildly terrified Wanda Weaver Yule met me in the hotel lobby, together with about a thousand other excited guests. The Chief gave me one swift look and drew the trooper to one side. Sideburns and Lennie were walking under their own power, but barely. I was between them, a hand on an arm of each, acting as a guide.

I got them outside and shoved them into the state patrol car. A few seconds later the trooper came out with his buddy. He nodded at me, telling me the prisoners would be down at state trooper headquarters if I wanted to interrogate them.

Wanda was at my elbow, grabbing my arm. Her green eyes were big with shock. "It's true, then? They were after me? To kill me?"

"What do you think, pet?"

Walrus-moustache rumbled, "Okay, let's clear out. I want some words with those murderers. You take Mrs. Yule home, Damon. Oh—nice work."

"Nice work?" Wanda screeched. "He saved my life!"

I had to go back inside for her ermine wrap, pushing a path through the crowd that had gathered. The reporters and photographers were shouting questions and popping flashbulbs all around us. Wanda decided she didn't want to be left alone, so she grabbed my hand and hung on while I barreled a path between notebooks and cameras.

It took us close to half an hour to be by ourselves in the Cadillac as I sent the speedometer needle edging up to twenty miles an hour on the dark country road. Wanda was shivering steadily, clinging to my right arm so I had to

61

drive with my left hand. From time to time she would reach across the wheel and grab that one, to kiss my bloodied knuckles. This was why I was driving so slowly. One wrong move at any speed faster than twenty and I'd have racked up the Caddy around a tree.

"Your poor dear hands," she kept whispering between kisses. "You saved my life, Rod, you actually did."

She acted as if this was a big surprise to her. When I reminded her it was my job, that it was the reason I didn't act as her escort to the mod ball, she almost wept.

"I know what you said, I just couldn't believe it," she muttered over and over. "I thought you d-didn't want to be seen in public with me."

"Don't be idiotic," I snapped. "You're a beautiful woman. Any male would be damn proud to be your escort."

She sniffled, "I feel like an old bag!"

"Well, you're not. Your only trouble is, you've got nothing to do to keep you busy. If you went back to the rodeo, you wouldn't have time to brood about your looks, you'd be too busy working to fret."

In a small voice, she said, "I've thought about it."

"Good. After this hassle is over, you can give all your time to it. I guess you can still ride a horse. So practice up a bit and maybe you can start a whole new life for yourself."

She snuggled closer, with her head on my shoulder. "Rod? Could you be a part of that new life?"

"Well, now, I do have a couple of jobs at the moment. I'm a sociology professor, founder and principal instructor for my League of Sexual Dynamics, and in my free hours I go to work on Coxe Foundation jobs like this."

"The rodeo would help me forget you," she murmured.

"Sure it would."

"The only trouble is, everything's been done before on the rodeo circuit," she pointed out. "I have to come up with a new gimmick, something completely different, because no matter what you say, Rod, I am past my peak. I just couldn't compete with those pretty girls in their bright satin blouses and frontier pants, with their little girl faces

62

bright and cheerful under those Stetsons."

"Sure you can," I protested.

"With a trick, yes," she nodded. "So they'd be more interested in the stunt than they are in how I look. I'll have to think about it."

We were almost at Heather Haven. It had taken us close to two hours to negotiate the fifty miles, what with all the hand-kissing and arm-hugging that had been going on. Wanda Weaver Yule was grateful to me, I must admit.

I turned the car into the drive. There were lights on in the house, I saw, and a big black limousine drawn up to one side of the high-columned front porch. A man in a chauffeur uniform was leaning against the front left fender, smoking a cigarette.

"Hi, Oliver," I called as I helped Mrs. Yule from the Cadillac. "The Chief inside?"

"He is—with Lucy."

"Who's Lucy?" snapped Wanda Weaver Yule.

"A girl who works for the Foundation."

She sniffed suspiciously but she walked through the front door and into the living room. Walrus-moustache was sitting gingerly in one of the love seats to the right of the wide marble fireplace. A pretty blonde in a miniskirted black velvet cocktail dress with black lace blouse under its tight bodice was slouched down in a pale gold satin sofa, long nyloned legs crossed high up.

"Where the hell've you been?" said Walrus-moustache.

"Driving home," I told him, glancing at Wanda, who was eyeing Lucy the same way the girl was regarding her.

The Chief growled at Wanda, "Maybe now you've gotten some sense about this case. This is Lucy Wells. She's going to be you for a while."

Wanda yelped in protest. I guess she figured Lucy and I would be carrying on the way she and I had been doing. My hand patted her hand.

"Relax, relax. What the Chief means is that she's going to pretend to be you, to draw the fire."

Lucy smiled, her green eyes going from me to Mrs. Yule. "I'll take your place in public, that is. When you have to go out, I go instead of you. If anybody wants to

63

kill you, they'll shoot at me instead."

"But you caught my killers," Wanda pointed out. "There's no more need to bother about protecting me." She thought a moment, then added weakly, "Is there?"

"We caught two men who tried to kill you," the Chief said. "We know from their own lips they were hired to do the job by a pretty girl with brown hair. They knew her only as Laura."

"Laura Ogden," I chipped in. "This means you aren't out of the woods yet, Mrs. Yule." I was being formal in front of Lucy Wells and old Walrus-moustache. I went on, "It's still most important that we protect you."

Wanda smiled into my eyes. "If you say so, Rod." Then she turned to look at the blonde girl. "You said you were to take my place in public?"

"Only in public," Lucy said, her eyes alight with mirth.

Wanda Weaver Yule asked, "When will you go to work?"

Lucy spread her hands. "Any time you say. Right now, if you'd like. I have blonde hair and green eyes, I can pass as you, I think. Dressed in your clothes, that is. If you don't mind."

"Oh, I don't mind. That was a pretty close call I had tonight. I've been fooling myself with the thought that when my motor exploded, it was an accident. Those men out there on the balcony were no accident."

"And you were their target," Walrus-moustache confirmed. "I questioned them, and they admitted they were there to do you in. The man with the gun is an expert marksman. He said he'd rather go to trial on an attempted murder charge than meet up with you again, Damon." He gave one of his rare smiles. "Can't say I blame him, after seeing what you did to them. You all right?"

I nodded. "Never better."

Wanda protested, "He is not! His poor knuckles are all bleeding. I'll have to doctor them before—before he goes to bed tonight."

Lucy asked innocently, "Should I sleep here?"

My hostess drew a deep breath. "Yes, I guess you'd better. I always take swims in the pool in the afternoon. You

64

can do that for me. And—er—sometimes I have to go see my lawyer from time to time. You can do that, carrying my written instructions."

Wanda Weaver Yule beamed, still clutching my arm. "We'll get along—as long as you confine yourself to the public appearances."

Lucy Wells smiled genially. She said, "I have a suitcase in the car. I'll go get it."

Walrus-moustache ran fingers through his hair. He was still wearing his pirate costume, and it was as Blackbeard that he said, "Thanks, Mrs. Yule. You won't regret cooperating with the Foundation. Between us, we'll not only save your life but get your would-be killers as well."

Lucy Wells and the Chief left the house.

Wanda said softly, "The maid can show Lucy to her room. You come upstairs with me. I'm feeling a need for protection."

It was more than protection that Wanda wanted.

CHAPTER FIVE

We made a very pleasant *ménage à trois* for the next four days. Lucy was Wanda Weaver Yule in public; she went to the law offices of Hutton, Hutton and Quinn; she took rides in the Shelby Cobra GT 500-KR; she swam in the estate pool, barely covered by an abbreviated bikini. In private, when she was alone in the Yule bedroom, she wore all the finest clothes. She played her part to the hilt.

Wanda herself was never seen outside the big house. This left her plenty of time to think up games that a lady boss and her chauffeur could play. It is a damn good thing I suffer from priapism because Wanda might otherwise have worn me out.

On the morning of the fifth day, there was a phone call for the real Wanda. She had to make a personal appearance in New York City. She was the donor of a school for orphans. It was some of her millions that had built the edifice, and now she must make an appearance at the school opening, when the mayor and a couple of other dignitaries were going to make speeches and other hoopla about the school.

"I feel strongly about that school," she said. "I've just got to go."

After some thought, I said, "So we'll go. The only thing is, we can't have you parading around like Wanda Weaver Yule. You've got to be somebody else, like a maid."

To my surprise, she nodded. "All right. I'll go along with that. Lucy can be me; I'll be her personal maid."

I chauffeured Lucy and Wanda north in the Cadillac.

66

Lucy lolled in the back, swathed in mink and jewels. Wanda sat beside me in her black outfit. It was a kind of joke to the millionairess.

"I'll have to appear myself at the ceremonies, you know," she told me on the way. "The trustees of the building fund know me very well. An imposter could never fool them."

"I'll drive Lucy there as you, then. You go as the maid. In the ladies' room you can change clothes."

"What about the suite?" Wanda asked.

"Yeah, the suite. So we'll make sure it's large enough for the three of us. Maybe a camp cot for me. You can sleep with Lucy."

She pouted, "That's no fun."

"For public consumption, you know. You have a built-in-excuse—these attempts on your life, you're terrified to be alone. Hell, the papers will eat it up."

The newspapers were full of the story. The Foundation made sure of that. Wanda Weaver Yule—the real one—gave out interviews in her home. If the object had been only to save her life, this would have been a stupid thing to do. But the Coxe Foundation was interested in tracking down the would-be killers and to do this the Opposition had to have a crack at killing her.

The suite at the Waldorf was lovely, with a view of the city eastward toward the river and Brooklyn. Below us, Lexington Avenue crawled with traffic. It was dusk, just turning into night, and the lights were coming on all over town.

Wanda and I stood together at one of the windows, looking out at one of the bridges connecting Manhattan island to Brooklyn. It was alive with lights, looking like a fairy structure against the blue velvet darkness.

"I'm hungry," she complained. "That sandwich at Howard Johnson's on the Jersey Turnpike seems like five days ago."

Lucy came in from the big bedroom. "I'll ring room service."

While she was at the phone, I got out a fast, Swiss-made Hasselbad camera from my valise. I was already wearing my shoulder holster, the butt protruding from under my left armpit. I felt we were ready for what might come.

Room service furnished us with three filet mignons, grilled over a charcoal fire, and three salads. None of us had any dessert but we did indulge ourselves with two pots of coffee. We chatted while we ate; we had become friendly by this time, all three of us.

Lucy stretched, yawning, "Me for bed. I'm beat."

Wanda nodded, "I'll be right in, Lucy. I'm tired myself." Her green eyes touched mine apologetically. I nodded. Hell, I was bushed too.

Lucy went into the bedroom, crossing to the vanity table. Wanda was just behind her, reaching for the zipper on her maid outfit. I was right at their heels.

Mrs. Yule paid me no nevermind, but Lucy sort of arched her eyebrows when she saw me lurking in the doorway. She was in the act of reaching for her skirt, to raise her dress up over her head.

"Must you?" she muttered.

"Line of duty, sweets. Suppose somebody were to snap off a shot at you while you had that dress up over your head?"

She said, "Oh, Rod, be reasonable."

But her voice was muffled because the red number she was wearing was rising past her chin. She made a nice picture in her long gun-metal nylons and the specially made slip trimmed with ivory lace. Her full hips wriggled a little, and she cursed softly when a lock of her golden hair caught in a zipper tooth.

I started forward. "I'll help——"

Whuppppp!

Lucy fell forward.

I whirled, the camera in my right hand lifting with instinctive reflex, aimed at the window. The camera had an infrared lens and an infrared flashbulb. There was no betraying light blast.

A woman hung in midair a yard from the window, a gun with a silencer in her hand. I got one long look at her while I was snapping the shutter release. "Midge Priest!" I breathed, and my fingers froze on the Hasselbad.

I could have reached for my gun when that surprise first wore off, but I chose to take another snapshot. A good thing I did, because a second after the camera clicked, she shot upward into the air.

I stuck my head out and looked up. Midge was rising roofward. Even as I yanked out my holstered revolver, she was stepping into another open window a few floors above. There was that same belt about her middle that she had worn the night she and Laura Ogden had levitated upward to the helicopter on the Outer Banks.

She was out of sight before the gun cleared my holster. I swung around, started to run across the room. If I could get upstairs before Midge could get down into the lobby, I could trap and capture her.

Wanda was yelling something at me. "Where are you going? Don't you realize she shot Lucy? My God! Give me a hand here."

She was trying to roll the girl over onto her back. I knelt, studied the red dress in which her head was still tangled, and her creamy shoulders, the back of her slip.

"There," I said, pointing. "The bullet hit there."

Wanda stared down at the unmarked slip. "You've got to be crazy! It would go through the slip and into her heart. Whoever did the shooting was a damn good shot."

"This is a special kind of nylon slip, honey. It's the same stuff as the boys in Viet Nam use to stop a bullet or a bayonet. The secret's in the weave, and has something to do with diverting the force of the impact as the bullet hits."

Lucy stirred. I said, "She's coming around. Lu, you okay?"

"I'm dead," she gasped.

I laughed, "You'll have a sore back, sure, but you'll be as good as new, come morning. Nice work, honey. I got two pictures. It was Midge Priest out there."

I waved a hand at the open window. "Out there."

Wanda snapped, "Oh, come off it. This suite is thirty floors above street level. There's no place for anybody to stand on or cling to."

"She was wearing some special kind of belt that lets her levitate, go up or down. She came down to shoot; she went up to escape."

"Oh, brother," breathed the millionairess.

Lucy was a limp weight as I got her to her feet, holding her against me for support. Wanda was muttering to herself as she untangled Lucy's hair from the zipper.

I bent and lifted Lucy, put her on the bed, face down. I raised the slip up to her bare shoulders. There was a faint black and blue mark on the pale white skin of her back. It would discolor even more in the hours ahead. I put a hand on her shoulder, shook her a little.

"Brave girl," I whispered.

She began to sob. "I—I'm n-not a brave g-girl," she stuttered. "I've b-been s-scared speechless these past few days. Wha-what if she'd aimed at m-my he-head?"

"Why, you poor, darling baby," Wanda cried, and leaned to take Lucy into her arms. "I never realized what this job assignment was doing to you. I thought you were one of those absolutely nerveless human beings whom I envy—and despise."

I dialed the boss-man. Walrus-moustache was in a suite not far from our own. The Chief was like the core of a labyrinth, with hundreds of contacts in all its many tunnels. He could make the Coxe Foundation jump when he yelled. I wanted him to yell.

"It was Midge Priest," I told him. "No mistake about it. I've got her face on film so you can show her picture to all our agents."

"I'll send a man down right away and have them developed inside the hour. You stay there just in case she makes another try."

"She won't," I assured him.

He listened while I described how the bullet intended to kill Lucy had hit her behind her heart, where the nylon slip protected her. "She's a bit weepy at the moment, but she's physically fine."

He told me he'd put in a call for a doctor, just to be on the safe side. "You get a good sleep, Damon. I may want you to follow that Priest woman only God knows where,

70

when we get a line of her. I'm sure she's going to report back to whoever it is that wanted Wanda Yule dead. To tell her mission accomplished and all that sort of thing."

During the next hour, a Foundation agent came for the film in my Hasselbad, a doctor appeared with his black kit in a hand and gave Lucy a thorough going-over, pronouncing her fit. He handed Wanda a salve she could massage into the skin, to alleviate any pain. Finally I went to bed.

I woke out of what seemed to be a drugged sleep to find Lucy in a thin nylon nightgown standing over me, shaking my arm. "It's the boss-man, it's the boss-man," she kept saying. "Rod, wake up."

My wristwatch told me it was three minutes past seven. "Don't you ever sleep?" I mumbled to the phone.

"Cheer up, Professor. I'm sending you to the Caribbean. You can loaf in the sun, you can ogle the girls, you only have to do one thing for me."

He sounded too damn cheerful. My heart sank.

"Midge is catching the four o'clock flight to Freeport on Grand Bahama Island by way of Eastern Airlines. You can be on the five o'clock flight to the same place."

"You've got to be kidding," I snarled. "All I have with me is a chauffeur's uniform."

"Tsk, tsk! Such unfaith in the Foundation. Your luggage will be aboard Flight 436. A man is on his way to your suite now with clothes for you to wear. Oh, by the way, you're to be a rich playboy. The man with your clothes will hand you fifty thousand dollars in cash. Have fun, Professor—and find out what the hell is going on!"

He hung up. I oozed back onto the couch.

I agreed with Walrus-moustache about one thing. What the hell *was* going on? I had nearly been killed; I had made love to three different women; I'd saved Wanda Weaver's life; I'd watched a girl shoot Lucy Wells in the back. For what reason?

Neither the Chief nor I knew why I was going through all this. Wanda Weaver Yule couldn't help us. The only way I could learn the answers was by flying to the Bahamas. I was so intrigued by the mystery of it all that I even gave up grumbling about my new assignment, as is my habit when Walrus-moustache calls me to put me on the spy spot.

I was even more anxious to go when a young man knocked on the door and handed me a new valise containing my traveling clothes and an envelope stuffed with fifty thousand dollars in spendable cash.

The clothes were something else again. One thing I give the boss-man, he never hedges when he sets out to spend money. I was to act the part of playboy and by God I was going to be a playboy, in his book. Saying goodbye to the girls, the playboy was on his way.

At Grand Bahama Island, the big jet tires down on the tarmac of Freeport Airport. It braked, its great jet engines throbbing. Then it began the taxi toward Customs.

A Foundation agent met me at Customs, issued me and my luggage through to a waiting taxi. He climbed into the taxi with me and brought me up to date as we drove along.

"Miss Priest has checked into the Beach hotel. We reserved a room for you, as well. We have three agents, two girls and a young man, to keep us informed of her every move. When they report in, you will be contacted.

"As I understand it, Miss Priest knows you. We don't want to give away the game by having her see you and get the wind up. You stay in your room until you hear from us. When she leaves the hotel, you can come out of your room."

"Some playboy I'm going to make." I groused.

His smile was sympathetic. "That was just old Walrus-moustache conning you. Part of his sales pitch. The only thing that keeps you going is that sometimes he tells the truth and you do have a good time. Best of luck on this one."

So I registered at the hotel, with a redhead who works for the Coxe Foundation assuring me that Miss Priest was already in her room. The telephone rang a short while later while I was shaving.

72

"The quarry is dining in the Crystal Room, Professor," said the redhead.

"I'll eat in my room," I promised. "Keep in touch."

There were no more phone calls until next morning. Then the bell jangled as I was studying my reflection in a mirror.

"The quarry is eating breakfast in the Waffle Bar," the redhead said.

"I'm getting tired of eating alone. Why don't you come up and share a platter of ham and eggs with me?"

A giggle, then: "No can do, Professor. Duty calls."

I sighed and hung up.

Midge Priest permitted me a little freedom an hour later when she left the hotel. I descended on the gambling hall attached to the hotel. I figured to try my luck a little, just to see what I could do with a hundred dollars.

I doubled my money at the blackjack table, and I took it as a good omen. I slid away from the gaming table.

A bellboy at the other side of the casino was yelling, "Professor Rod Damon, calling Professor Rod Damon."

I tipped him a buck and followed him to a phone booth. The redhead was on the other line.

"The quarry has been buying underwater swimming gear, Professor. She's heading for Shark Point. May I suggest you do the same? You'll find a blue Marcos 1600 in the hotel parking lot. Its yours for the duration. There is special gear in the trunk, including a face-mask, aqualung and flippers. Bon Voyage."

I just had to meet redhead. She was so efficient!

The Marcos 1600 is a British-built car in the sporty category, with fancy, sleek lines. Mine was a real honey, with buttons instead of door handles, wire wheels, the works. I slid onto the black leather seat with a sigh of comfort. I was positive Redhead would have put a map of the island into the glove compartment. The map was there.

The Marcos 1600 will do a hundred and twenty miles an hour. I just eased her up to eighty on the straights and let her slip around the curves at a mild forty. She held to

73

the road as if there was leech blood in her paint.

I found Shark Point without too much trouble.

A gorgeous girl with skin the color of light mahogany decorated a beach blanket in a bikini bathing suit that hid only the absolute essentials of her curving body. As I braked the blue bolt which the automotive industry calls a car, she rose to her feet and came running toward me. She had red hair.

I met her halfway, caught her in my arms and kissed her soft red lips. She was startled, but she gave back the caress after a moment of hesitation. Her mouth tasted like honey, her properly curved body gave to my squeeze.

"Well!" she sort of gasped.

"Well? Hell, it was perfect. Let's do it again."

She giggled as her eyebrows tried to frown. "I didn't come here for hanky-panky, Professor. The quarry's on its way—out there."

Reluctantly I pried my eyes away from the twin brown mounds half in and half out of the cups of her bikini halter to follow her pointing finger. She seemed to be showing me the entire Atlantic Ocean, all the way to the United States mainland.

"Don't tell me she's on her way to keep a date in Florida," I murmured.

"Your job is to find out exactly where she's going."

"Yeah," I assented glumly. The sunlight felt so good and the female flesh against me was so exciting that I was in no mood for a swim. I should have remembered Redhead was very efficient. She freed herself gently, as if to remind me that Uncle Sam needed me more than she did at this moment. She even gave me a pinch over my belt, hard, to bring me back from my thoughts.

I went over to the Marcos and opened the trunk. Redhead was right. Gear of all kinds—swimming apparatus, harpoon guns, a couple of revolvers, powerful binoculars—met my stare. If a spy needed it on a job, it was in that trunk.

With Redhead helping me, I grabbed a Healthways dive mask, a Scubaire 300 regulator that Redhead attached to

74

a twin tank assembly for me while I was shucking off my clothes.

I stripped down to my skin. We were all alone out here. Shark Point is a kind of lonely spot, which was why Midge Priest chose it, I imagine. There was nobody around but Redhead and me.

Her long-lashed eyes grew big as they took my manhood in at a quick glance. The bare mounds under her bikini cups lifted upward as she drew a deep breath.

"Well!" she breathed, then added quickly, "I mean perfect."

I grinned as I stuffed my male ornaments into the wetsuit. Redhead sighed, knelt down and slipped a pair of fins on my feet.

She fitted the assembly tanks to my back, tightened its harness. I grabbed the goggles and was ready for business. Redhead walked me to the water's edge.

"Anything special I need to know?" I wondered.

"I'm your date, if anyone comes down here before you're back. You love underwater swimming. You're going out to examine the coral growths on this section of the Grand Bahama banks."

"Okay, date." I smiled as I leaned to kiss her cheek. When she looked a little puzzled, I added, "In case anybody's watching through field glasses. We secret agents must be on guard at all times."

I waded out and submerged.

For half an hour I swam in the general direction in which the redhead had pointed. The thought touched my mind from time to time that Midge Priest could be within thirty feet of me, and I'd never know it. Needles in haystacks had nothing on me.

Then I saw a pale light up ahead.

I swam toward it. Up close, I found this was a battery-powered submarine lamp, very low in candlewatts so that it would not be visible from the surface. I made out a number on it: 3.

I was in the middle of a vast forest of elkhorn coral, great jutting spines that resembled the huge horns of the

75

Canadian elk. Seaweeds of varying colors swayed back and forth near them, and moving lazily through those fronds came the torpedo body of a trumpet fish. To one side, I glimpsed convoluted brain corals.

I realized I was somewhere in an underwater maze that was Midge Priest's destination. Whoever she worked for apparently had money to spend on fripperies such as this, to insure safe meeting places.

I swam on, hunting for light number 4.

There is an Underwater Trail much like this one in the waters off the Virgin Islands. You get into your snorkel and your swimsuit, and you start where a blue and white sign reads BEGIN UNDERWATER TRAIL. You soon find yourself in a fantasy of brain coral and sea anemone, where plastic-sealed plaques set into rocks act as guides, telling you that you are observing antler coral or a school of parrot fish that live in the lagoon.

The trail I was following was not for the public. It was a labyrinth of bright scarlet fire sponges, golden coral, branching stalks of club coral, beds of brilliantly colored sponges and clusters of stinging coral. And at any moment a member of the Opposition might decide to use my body as a bull's-eye for an underwater harpoon.

The wet-suit kept me warm, but there was an annoying tingle down my spine as I swam like a ghost through the greenish light. I could see reasonably well in the clear waters, and I was sure the Other Side was able to do the same.

The little lamps came and went. I noticed the lamps were leading inward into a forest of antler coral, where the going got tight. I scraped my sides half a dozen times on razorsharp edges, and thanked my lucky stars the Coxe Foundation had not made me take this route in just a pair of swim trunks.

Deeper into the maze I went.

It was dark down there. Number 9 light had faded into invisibility and I was forced to use my hands to guide me through the narrow apertures between the coral prongs.

Then it all opened up.

76

Midge Priest was in an open space between towering coral formations, holding what appeared to be a slip of paper to a greenish lamp. I waited, suspended in the water, watching her.

She gave a little nod with her head and ripped the paper into four pieces. She cast it to the undersea currents, then looked up. There was an opening in the hedge of elkhorns above her. With a kick of her flippered feet she rose upward, swimming gracefully.

I waited until her swimsuited body had vanished before I moved from my hiding place into the hollow. My eyes saw two of the torn pieces settling to the bottom; I went for them, caught them and rolled them up.

The first touch of those torn bits told me this was not paper, but thin rubber. I found the third piece caught on a branch of the elkhorn coral; I removed it very gingerly. I was afraid the ink on the thin rubber membranes would run in the sea water after exposure, so I tucked the pieces inside my belt. Then I began my hunt for the last section.

It could not have gone far. Midge had made no attempt to hide it, she had just cast it away. I spent five minutes searching before I felt a faint submarine current moving between the coral growths. I followed it into a crevice and there was the missing piece.

I rose up through the hole as Midge had done. I did not go to the surface for fear she would be there, swimming ahead of me. I leveled off about five yards below and started stroking.

Naturally, I didn't want to go up onto the beach just yet. Midge would be there ahead of me, and it was no part of my plan to show myself at this stage of the game.

Fifty yards from shore, I stopped, treading water. I removed the goggles and let my head rise just above the surface. I swept the beach with my eyes. Redhead was sitting alone on her blanket, clasping her arms. Midge was nowhere in sight. I went in with a brisk Australian crawl stroke.

Redhead came to meet me, walking with a strut that swung her hips. I told myself I had to have some of that

77

before my stay in the Bahamas was over.

When I was half out of the swimsuit, she asked, "How'd it go?"

"Good. What about Midge? You see her?"

"She didn't show here. You don't think she swam the other way, do you? To meet a boat?"

"I hope the hell not. Here, let's see."

I got out the thin rubber strips, I patched them together with the girl leaning over my left shoulder as we knelt together on her blanket.

The note read: *Tomorrow night, the* Albatross. *Ten. Twenty-seven. Seventy-nine.*

It was that simple.

"What's it mean?" asked the redhead.

My shoulders shrugged, brushing her right breast with my left. She moved back a little. "Who knows?" I asked. "Maybe it's some sort of secret dating service. But all kidding aside, I've got to be there. Ten is probably the time. The other numbers probably represent the latitude and longitude. I've got to get hold of a nautical map."

"The one thing I didn't put in the trunk," Redhead nodded.

I got up, lifting her to her feet. "We'll go back to the hotel. You get that map and join me in my room. We'll study it together."

"What, no etchings?" she murmured. "Sorry about that, Professor. I do have a job, which doesn't include shenanigans in a fellow worker's room."

"Even if he needs your company very much?"

She laughed, shaking her red hair.

So I went by my lonesome back to my room. I wondered why Midge Priest was going out to twenty-seven by seventy-nine. She had murdered Wanda Weaver Yule—or so she thought—so it might just be she was going to join her companions in the Opposition. I had no way of knowing. It was all guesswork.

Redhead knocked on the door at ten minutes past four. She slipped into the opening I made when I opened the door, with a furtive air. Over her shoulder she wore a bag.

The map was in the bag, she showed me, lifting it out. She was a chic chick in a black and white tunic dress in which a big rhinestone pin was fastened. Her red hair was coiffeured into a dazzling upsweep holding dozens of tiny pearls on long hairpins.

"You changed your mind," I said. "You've come to share dinner in my room."

"Uh-uh. No. I came to hand you the map."

She slammed the map into my palm.

"Hey," I exclaimed as she opened the door. "What about our next contact? I have to make plans. You damn well don't expect me to swim out to twenty-seven seventy-nine!"

She halted, then closed the door, not wanting to be seen standing in my open doorway talking to me for fear the Opposition might get suspicious.

"You do have a point there," she murmured.

Her eyes questioned me. I went to the night table, spread out the map. I sat down on the bed to study it, turning on the bed lamp. My forefinger went to a point about fifteen miles north of the westernmost point of Grand Bahama Island.

"Is there a boat rental place around here?"

She nodded. "Just outside Freeport."

"I've got to rent a small submarine, if it's possible. One of those two-man jobs." I grinned. "Love to have you come along, Red."

"Uh-uh. I don't think you'll be able to rent a sub. There is one, it's true, a second-hand job the Harbor Rental Company bought when the United States Navy auctioned off some of its surplus stock. I've seen it docked at the quay, but I've never known anyone who was able to rent it."

"They just didn't offer enough money. You watch. I'll go rent it right now, while Midge is still in her room. She is in her room, isn't she?"

"Taking a nap."

"How do you find out things like that?"

She smiled. "Disguised as a cleaning lady."

There was no more reason for her to stay, she told me,

so she would leave. I sighed and stared at her hips pressing into the white stuff of her tunic dress. The door opened and closed. I sighed again.

I drove to Freeport in the blue Marcos. After asking directions from a policeman, I moved down to the harbor road and the smell of salt water. A dozen cabin cruisers swung to the lift and swell of the tide on their anchor chains. Further out was a big Diesel-engine yacht, all white with polished brass fittings. Its name read: *Albatross.*

With a sense of accomplishment, I sauntered around the docks and pilings. In a little while Midge Priest would be keeping a date with that big yacht. I marveled at the care the Opposition took not to make contacts when there was any chance of being seen, and wondered at the secretiveness of the head man.

Whoever he was, he took no risks.

My study of the *Albatross* complete, I turned to enter the boat rental company offices, a squat white building with buoys, with some lobster pots thrown in for good measure.

Midge Priest was standing at the counter.

CHAPTER SIX

She was too busy yakking with the wizened old man behind the counter to see me. I ducked sideways into the nettings, out of sight of the doorway. My heart was slamming away; it had been a near thing.

I walked down onto one of the quays projecting out into the harbor. I sat down on a pile of rope so I could watch the little Sprite parked a dozen yards from my Marcos 1600. It was the only other car in the lot, so it must belong to Midge. I smoked a cigarette, slowly.

She came out without a glance at her surroundings. She climbed into the Sprite and started the engine. I waited until she was gone about five minutes before I stood up from the rope coils and walked toward the building.

The man with the leathery brown skin bobbed his head at sight of me. "Do something for you, guv'nor?"

"I want to rent a two-man submarine."

The little man blinked. "Sorry, mate. It ain't for rent. Belongs to the company. We use it to do a bit of undersea mining at times."

My wallet came into view. I opened it and drew out two five-hundred-dollar bills, American money. I watched the old man with the captain's cap perched on the back of his head as he ran a tongue around his lips.

"One thousand dollars," I murmured. "Does your mining operations earn as much over a twenty-four-hour period?"

"Well, now. Can't say as it does."

I might have argued, but this was Foundation money, I drew out a third bill and placed all three carefully on the counter. The greed in the eyes staring at these riches was easy to read.

"Fifteen hundred for using your submarine tonight and

81

maybe part of tomorrow. If you don't want it, okay by me."

I put out a hand to take back the bills. His leathery hand covered mine like a leech. "Hold now, hold now. Didn't say I wouldn't do it, did I, mate? Mining isn't all that good around these parts."

He put the three bills into a cash register, cackling laughter. "Tell the truth, we ain't done much mining to speak of. I've always been meaning to, but never got around to it."

"Where's it docked?"

He made me come along with him along a quay. Up ahead I saw a sleek Century inboard runabout roped to a piling. I paused. "Hmmm. Maybe I ought to rent that Coronado. It looks fast. I could dive to make the explorations I want."

"Can't do it, mate. The Century's rented."

"Oh? That girl I just saw?"

He chuckled, walking past the inboard bumping the rubber half-tires wired to the pilings. "Maybe she wants a bit of fun tonight. There's to be a full moon."

"He's a lucky man," I smiled.

"Aye, that he is . . . but here's your submersible."

The submarine was an old version of a research submersible built by General Dynamics for some big university, the man told me. Modern scientific discoveries had outdated it, but its yellow and blue hull was still capable of submerging safely to a six-hundred-foot depth, and of staying submerged for close to ten hours. It could move at a speed of three to four knots the hour.

"They've got new ones can go down fifteen thousand feet and work under pressures of seven thousand pounds the square inch. But I don't imagine you need one of them."

"This will do nicely," I admitted.

My eyes touched the Century Coronado, which was capable of hitting a forty-four miles an hour speed. To get to where Midge Priest was going tonight, I'd have to take off well before she did. I glanced at my wristwatch.

"Tell you what," I said to the old man. "Fill her up, get

82

her ready. I'll be back inside the hour to take her out."

"You pay for the petrol," he reminded me.

I peeled off a century note and let him fold his wrinkled fingers around it. "You do a good job getting it in tiptop shape and that hundred-dollar bill is all yours, above and beyond the cost of the gas. Or petrol, as you call it."

His eyes glinted greedily.

He had the submersible ready when I came back. I was wearing slacks and rubber-soled sports shoes, a turtleneck shirt and sports jacket. Inside the shoulder holster was a spring fun that would fire a drugged pellet with only a slight whooshing sound. I didn't want gunfire to alert the whole world if I ran into trouble out there.

I went down through the hatch into a small cabin where two seats sat side by side above twin viewing ports. The controls were close to hand. I looked up at the wizened face peering down at me.

"You know how to operate this thing?" he wondered.

"Like my canoe back home," I grinned.

The vertical propulsion motor started with a roar, as if to prove the truth of what I said. The man nodded and swung the hatch closed. I reached up and locked it tight. The old man would throw off the ropes.

I opened the valves to flood the main ballast tank.

In half an hour I was heading under thirty feet of water toward the Atlantic Ocean, fifteen miles off the west end of the Grand Bahama Island. It was noisy inside the old submersible. And dark. I dared not switch on any lights, outside maybe the flashlight hooked onto my belt so I could read the nautical map in my jacket pocket.

I chugged along at three knots the hour.

It took me close to five hours to reach my destination at that speed. It got damn boring after a time, especially since I didn't even dare to take a look at the surface. Even the sight of a shark would have been welcome. I let myself dream about how much fun it would be if Redhead was in the empty seat beside me.

Imagine parking and smooching under the surface of the Atlantic Ocean, with no fuzz around to send you on your way! The mere idea sent a raw chill of desire through me. I would have turned the lights on for that. Love-making, like smoking, is best done in the light.

When I was as close as my calculations told me I could get to twenty-seven and seventy-nine, I shut off the motors and hung there in the water. My watch told me it was about quarter to ten. I waited for ten minutes, then took off my clothes. Under them I was wearing swim trunks.

I raised the submersible then.

She popped from the water about half a mile from the *Albatross*, riding its anchor in the moonlit darkness. The yacht was alive with electric lights shedding their radiance out across the waters. The brightness did not reach my body as I clambered out of the hatch, listening for the sound of the Coronado motor.

I was west of the yacht, invisible in the darkness. The submersible had no anchor, but I figured the thing would stay roughly in the same position while I swam across to the *Albatross*.

My body slid down into the water.

I was halfway across to the yacht when my ears picked up the sound of a 225 horsepower V8 engine. The Century Coronado boasts such a motor, so I figured Midge Priest was approaching to keep her rendezvous with the *Albatross*.

By the time I got to the huge white hull, Midge was already aboard. Me, I climbed up the anchor chain and hung there, wet and cold, while I waited to pick up voices. It was quiet, this far out to sea, and sound carries easily.

"—make such a decision," said a velvety voice completely unfamiliar to me. "It shows how smart you are, Midge. You could go far in the organization. Very far. But you want to call it quits, and that's all right too."

"I was afraid you wouldn't want me to, Doctor."

That was Midge Priest's voice, no doubt about it. I tightened my grip on the chains and raised by body slowly until I was scanning the foredeck. There had been a nervous tremelo in her throat that told me Midge was scared witless.

"Don't be ridiculous," murmured velvet-voice. I could get a brief glimpse of her as she sat with crossed legs un-

84

der a short-sleeved shift dress striped in brown and beige from hem to the somewhat large turtleneck. Her brown hair was done in a bun at the back of her head, she wore glasses, and her hands toyed with a brown leather handbag. Despite the rather handsome curves of her mature body, she looked like a high school physics teacher.

She was saying, "We don't run our little establishment like a police state, you know. You want out, you can go out, with our thanks and with the money I promised you for a job well done."

She lifted a hand from her bag, snapping its fingers.

A girl stepped out of the shadows, and I did a double-take. Shades of Barbarella! This dame with the feather-cut blonde hair was attired in a uniform of sorts—and what sorts! It was of black satin, tight to her hips, breasts and thighs. It was so tight that I thought at first I was seeing a naked Negress. Her tanned face beneath the blonde hair dispelled that notion.

Around her curving hips was a leather belt with a holstered automatic. The automatic bobbed on her hips in tune with the breasts bobbing up above. She had a dazzling smile which she showed to Midge. She held an envelope in her hands.

She handed the envelope to the older woman.

Velvet-voice counted out some bills, showing them to Midge, who was all eyes as she stared down at the crisp greenbacks. They went back inside the envelope and the woman handed it to her.

"There you are, my dear. I want to wish you all the luck in the world in your future life. I don't have to ask you if you're going to keep a tight lip about our little venture, and about our organization."

"Oh, yes, I will. I will!" Midge vowed.

She sounded as if she could not believe her ears, that despite her brave front, she was positive she was going to be in trouble. She seemed to freeze in her mingled relief and despair, leaning forward slightly toward the older woman. Her hands about the envelope tightened until the paper crumpled.

The woman doctor rose to her feet, patting Midge gently on her shoulder. "I'll be leaving now. I'll send your motorboat back to the dock. You'll stay on only just so long as the *Albatross* can put you wherever you want to go."

"I—I had thought of taking a vacation on the island."

"In that case, spend the night on board. Or if you want, leave now. But be good enough to see me to the tender. I have to be off myself on a matter of business tonight in Freeport."

"Whatever you say, Doctor."

Midge walked with the older woman toward the port rail. She stood there leaning on the railing as the doctor walked down the ship's ladder to the tender, which must have been butting moldboards with the Century Coronado. The girl in the skintight uniform stood slightly behind Midge, also looking down.

I threw a leg up over the starboard rail, where it passed over the brass fairlead through which the anchor chain ran to the windlass. My bare feet made no sound as I put them firmly on the deck.

Midge Priest could answer questions. If she remained on the *Albatross*, I had to find a way to reach her cabin and abduct her, if necessary. If she told me what I wanted to know, fine. Then I would dive overside and swim back to my little submersible.

The uniformed girl put a hand to her belt.

There was a small automatic in the holster hanging on the belt. She was lifting the automatic from the holster as the tender roared into life on the far side of the yacht.

"Midge! Duck!" I bellowed, and leaped.

My voice startled Midge, who turned and stared at me, but she couldn't recognize me because of my mask. The girl flunky also whirled, her eyes getting big at sight of me. The hand holding the automatic at her side came out of its paralysis. The gun lifted toward my all but naked body.

Suddenly the gun veered, turned on Midge.

The blonde girl had been gaping at me, not believing what she saw. When the uniformed girl turned her gun toward her, I yelled.

86

"She's going to kill you, Midge!"

I was still too far away to interfere. Midge grabbed for the gun, the gun went off and I held my breath as I ran those last few yards between the struggling girls and my speeding body.

Out of the corners of my eyes I saw three more girls in those skintight uniforms come racing from a deck cabin. They ran for me. Ahead of me, Midge and her companion were locked in a desperate struggle, bumping into the port rail, sliding sideways across the deck into a stanchion.

I angled my run toward the three girls.

My feet went off the deckplanks.

I dove into the girls sideways, like a Green Bay blocking back clearing a path for his runner. The girls screeched as they slammed backwards, thumping onto the deck and sliding.

I scrambled for them, grabbing a gun from one and hurling it, kicking a second gun from another. The third girl had slammed into a rail with her head. She lay motionless.

Ignoring her, I ran for Midge and the girl with whom she was struggling. My hand shot forward for the automatic. I gripped it, twisted. The girl screamed in pain as her fingers tore from the savagery of my wrench. I threw the gun overboard.

I only hit women in self-defense, or while defending another person. My left fist traveled eight inches. It landed on the side of a jaw. The girl's head spun sideways, her knees buckled and she slumped down, her dead weight tearing her wrist free of Midge's grip.

"Come on," I yelled at the blonde girl.

"You!" she gasped. "Where'd you—you're dead!"

I gave her a slap on her buttock. "Get the hell over that starboard rail—fast!"

The two girls without automatics were coming for us. The girl who still held the automatic in her hand was reviving, shaking her head and stirring with her legs.

"Go, Midge—go!"

She caught the urgency in my voice. She ran for the rail. I turned back toward the oncoming Valkyries. One I hit

87

with a fist right in the middle of her belly between her rib-case and her navel. She doubled up with a sickening gasp, and started retching even before she hit the deck.

The second girl tried to brake her run. I reached for her. I was aiming at her arm, to grip it and hurl her, but when she braked I missed my target. My spread-fingered hands closed down on her breasts.

She was the tomboy type and didn't have too much up front, but what there was, I fastened on with the grip of a steel vise. She screamed as the pain rocketed through her body, that began bucking in reflex response to my grip.

Both hands fastened to her breasts, I moved sideways, hurling her with my hands tight on her young breasts, across the deck. She went through the air like an aerialist falling off a tightrope. Her head and neck rammed into the side of the cabin. I winced at the dull thud.

Midge was at the rail, grabbing it and leaping upward to clear it. I got a glimpse of nyloned legs and bare thighs as her skirt flared, then she was dropping out of sight toward the water.

I disdained the rail. I took a long leap, diving over that brass bar, arms together as my body went down. It was lucky for me I did. A bullet raced me through the darkness. It grazed my calf as I went into my dive. If I'd hesitated to lay hands to the rail and vault over as Midge Priest had done, that lead pellet would have hit the middle of my back.

I fell for the black waters. Midge was nowhere in sight. I hit the cold, dark wetness and went under.

I swam underwater for about fifty feet before I had to surface for air. Midge was slightly behind me, treading water.

"What are you doing?" I rasped. "That girl with the gun is hanging over the rail looking for us."

"I can't swim in this dress! It's got to go."

She wriggled and writhed and in a moment I caught a look at her sodden garment moments before it vanished in the water. "I kicked off my shoes back a ways," she panted, turning to swim.

I saw a pink behind under wet, tissue-thin panties as

she began to swim away from the yacht. Since she was moving in the general direction of the submersible, I let her go, and flicked a glance at the *Albatross.*

The girl with the automatic in her hand was steadying it with both hands, elbows resting on the rail. She had just sighted us swimming, now she was zeroing in with the Colt.

"Dive!" I yelled at Midge, and went down myself.

I swam under the surface for a dozen yards. I surfaced and looked back at the yacht. The girl had snapped off a shot. I heard something hit the water with a screeching whine, but she had lost sight of us. I drew a deep breath when I saw no sign of Midge, and dove again.

We made it in slow stages to the submersible. When we were a hundred yards from the *Albatross,* I judged it safe enough to swim on the surface where we could make better time. I was damn cold and I knew Midge must be freezing in just her underthings.

"Got a two-man sub ahead," I told her as we swam. "Just keep going and you can't miss it."

She didn't bother to nod. Her bare arms kept stroking, her stockinged feet went on beating. The submersible looked real good to me, its yellow superstructure like a welcome home light in the faint radiance from the yacht's lights.

I put a hand to her elbow, aided the all but exhausted girl up onto the tiny deck. This research craft was no luxury submarine, it had no rail and its deck was curved. Midge slipped and floundered her way forward as I hoisted myself out of the water and went to aid her in getting the hatch raised.

Her teeth were chattering as she slid a shapely stockinged leg over the hatch rim and found the tiny ladder. Her breasts bobbled under a cobwebby brassiere as she swung about to grasp the rim and fumble with a foot for the rungs.

She lifted her eyes for an instant before she ducked her head out of view to look at me in something like awe. "I'm saving my questions until I get warm," she chattered, and went down out of sight.

89

I dropped after her, closed the hatch, locked it in place.

We gave ourselves a couple of minutes to get our wind back, and to do something about our cold flesh. Midge was crouched with her arms about herself, not to protect her breasts from my stare but to try and squeeze some heat into her bloodstream. There was gooseflesh on her soft thighs above the ripped stockings. I noticed that she had tucked the envelope with her money inside the stocking on her right leg.

"Now you know," I growled, turning to lift my sports jacket and shirt and put them within reach of her hand, "what sort of outfit you were working for."

There was a towel in the Eastern Airlines bag I had carried onto the submersible, together with a hammered silver hip flask containing some expensive Pinwinnie Scotch. I handed the towel to Midge.

"Get those wet things off and dry yourself. Then you can have a swig of this Scotch."

Midge reached behind her back to get at the brassiere snaps. Her breasts swung forward, swaying slightly. I let my eyeballs feast on those sleek white weights with their cold-hardened brown nipples. Midge Priest had marvelous breasts. I congratulated myself on having saved them for all the males in the world who would get to see them, some day.

She asked, "Now I know—what?"

"You know you're dealing with a bunch of solid gold heels. They pay you off for trying to murder Wanda Weaver Yule, then they try to kill you and take the money back. Great bunch, all right."

"For trying to kill Wanda Weaver Yule? I did kill her. I saw her fall." Midge was shivering while she ran the big towel over her naked breasts. She had forgotten her garterbelt, panties and stockings that were dripping wet.

I was damn cold myself, but I knelt down and unfastened her garters and slid her nylons down. The wet envelope with its greenbacks I handed up to her. She tossed it to one side.

"You only thought you killed her," I told her, and explained how the whole thing had been a trap.

90

She was silent for a few minutes while I eased the stockings off. I was reaching for her panties when I realized the submersible was still above the surface.

"Oooops! I have things to do, honey."

I opened the valves to the main ballast tank. The reassuring gurgle of incoming water told me that we would be submerging in a few seconds. I waited until the gauges showed me we were at the sixty-foot mark. Then I closed the valves. The submersible would hang here while I finished the job of stripping Midge Priest.

I went back to her. She had not changed position, she just stood there shivering with the towel wrapped about her above the navel. I knelt down. Through the wet transparency of her panties I could see her golden pubic hairs. I sighed and fastened my fingers in the panty elastic.

Down came the panties. Up went her left leg so I could draw her foot through the leg opening. Then the right leg lifted. I draped the panties over a valve handle.

"How did you get out of the cellar?" she whispered.

I explained about that while I was removing her garterbelt. Naked, she posed for me as I knelt before her like a slave.

"I'm glad," she said when I was finished. "I didn't want to kill you. I thought that leaving you locked up would be enough. It was Laura who insisted."

I took the towel and rubbed its fluffiness over her hips. "After that, you hired two hoodlums to ·kill Wanda Weaver Yule at the country club."

She nodded, eyes wide. "You tumbled to that?"

I grinned, slapping her flank so she would turn and show me her bare buttocks. I dried them slowly, watching the soft flesh shake to my ministrations. She was looking back over her left shoulder at me while I went on talking.

"I was acting as her bodyguard."

When her buttocks were dry, I leaned forward and kissed her on each cheek. Midge giggled and pushed her softness back into my face.

"You'd better stop that. I'm feeling pretty grateful to you right now and it wouldn't take much to turn me on."

I dried the backs of her thighs and calves. Then I told

91

her to turn and face me. Her soft white belly made an outward bulge below her navel. I ran the towel over it.

"Did you hear what I said?" she smiled, moving her thighs together. Her hand touched the back of my head, urging me forward.

"I heard; I'm not made of wood."

I kissed her bellyflesh. She hissed breath in between her teeth. I whispered against her skin, "This is a case of business before pleasure, sweets."

She sighed and drew back, giving her loins to the towel in my fingers. I dried her slowly, carefully. Her voice murmured, "I suppose you want to know everything. Well, I don't owe any loyalty to Doctor Howard—not after what she tried to do to me. I'll tell you anything you want to know."

I dried her feet last.

Then I got to my own feet and stripped off my bathing trunks. Midge stared, saying, "Oh, yes! You *are* excited."

"It's my priapism," I chuckled.

"Oh, yes. You mentioned that last time we met. Still bothered by it, aren't you? I'm glad."

I dried myself and reached for my shorts.

Midge was there ahead of me, drawing my Jockeys away from my fingers. Her face was gleeful as she stared down at me. "Oh, now, it's so nice and warm in here—don't let's cover up."

"Who is Doctor Howard?" I asked.

She giggled, reaching for me. Her hand was warm and soft as it surrounded my personal problem. "Do you want to talk business?" she whispered.

"I'm afraid I do, hon. To tell the truth, I'm dying of curiosity. How in hell did you and Laura levitate up to that helicopter?"

"You saw that, did you? Oh—from the cellar window. We were wearing anti-gravity belts. You know, like in the science-fiction stories."

"It figured to be something like that," I remarked drily. "You were wearing one when you shot our girl agent in the Yule suit at the Waldorf too."

"I was."

92

Midge was sinking down to a squatting position in front of me. She let go her grip only long enough to play her long red fingernails across my groin in that tickling process the erotic experts call "playing at spiders' legs." My body shuddered to the pleasure she was feeding into my flesh.

"Still want to talk business?" she murmured.

"I do." Curse my will power, I thought. "Did Doctor Howard invent it?"

"Oh, my no. Harold Hayes Yule was the inventor."

"Who?" I screamed.

Midge looked up at me, her hands feathery as they stilled their movements. Her eyes were open wide in surprise. "Why, yes. Wanda's husband. He was an electronics genius, you know. He inherited his textiles business, I've been told, but he invented a couple of machines that worked electronically to speed up a few processes and improve the method of weaving, that tripled his millions."

Her fingers went on moving.

To her fingernails she added the fillip of a moist tongue dragging across my swollen flesh. Her gurgling laugh told me she heard my gasp and stifled moan. I stared down at her pouting red mouth, the saliva-glistening tonguetip.

"Easy," I growled. "Easy, there."

"Liar! You want it hard. Like this!"'

I groaned, shaking all over. Nobody could resist the treatment Midge Priest was giving me. I tried to be stoical about it, I reached up and gripped the iron steel struts that strengthened the rounded hull. I sought to pull away from her hands and mouth. I lacked the ability, I found. Instead, I was thrusting my hips forward.

"I won't tell you any more," she murmured. "I'm going to be like a Sphinx when it comes to talking about the organization. Unless you cooperate, darling."

"Yeah," I breathed. "Yeah, I guess you won't."

I took a handful of her long blonde hair and yanked her head back. I leaned down and kissed her with open lips. Our tongues toyed together in that artful caress known as the *ferame* by the Arabs, in which the tongue of the male trades places with that of the female, while the female tongue remains within the male mouth.

93

Midge added a new spice to this *ferame*. My penis had lodged in the vale between her bulging breasts by my bent-over position. Midge brought her hands up and caught her breasts in her palms, shoving them together, entrapping my manhood. Slowly and lazily she rubbed her breasts together against me, as Ottavia did to her lovers as recorded by Aloysia Sigaea in her Dialogues.

Her palms left her bulging breasts, slipped forward onto my rockhard thighs and traveled upward. My own hands went beneath her armpits, drew her from her squatting position to a standing one. Naked, we pressed our loins together, her soft belly pillowing itself against my muscled front, her thighs moving lazily against my most sensitive spot.

Midge was moaning, head back so her long blonde hair fell down to the rise of her plump buttocks. My hands were stroking her back from her shoulders to those quivering buttocks. When my fingers grasped her behind, she opened her lips and cried out in her delight.

"Please," she whimpered. "Please, Rod—please!"

"Have you ever formed the way of the monkey on a stick?"

"No. Ohhh, no! But do it—do it!"

My hands under her arms lifted her. She sensed what I would do, her hand went down to clasp and guide me as I lowered her. When she rested on me, fitting me as the piston does the cylinder, Midge gasped, wriggling. Her breathing through her wide-open mouth was that of a bellows.

"Put your feet on the backs of my knees," I directed, bending my legs slightly. I felt the scrape of an instep on my calf, then her right foot slipped into its living stirrup. The left foot planted itself.

Midge cooed, understanding bursting inside her with the pleasure our genitals aroused in each other. Her soles gave her a purchase on my legs, she could raise and lower herself with ease, as one raises and lowers a toy monkey on a stick. Up and down, up and down, without a break or pause in the rhythm of her movement.

94

"This must be—hard on you," she sobbed, convulsing in her ecstasy.

"It is," I said, panting slightly. "A man has to be in pretty good shape for this one."

"Why not—make it easier?"

I walked her contorting body to the pilot seat of the submersible. I sank downward as Midge unlocked her legs. The seat was low. She could thrust her legs through the seat-arm openings so her soles rested flat on the cabin floor.

"I've never made love underwater before," she gasped. "We're in a little world all our own. We could be the only ones on Earth."

She swung her hips to invisible music.

Her hips were performing that quivery, side to side motion of the hula dance, the flesh jiggling in tiny ripples as her movements grew faster, faster. I don't know whether a female has ever danced the hula on your body, but believe me, this is an experience.

"You are to watch the hands," she breathed, hips sliding back and forth in that jerk-jerk-jerk rhythm which somehow pulses with the heartbeat of the onlooker. "Not the breastworks. The hands tell the story. The hips and feet just beat out the rhythm."

"Yeah," I moaned. Whatever you say, honey."

"The word is *wahine u'i*. That means a really gorgeous girl. Or you could say, *oluolua,* man, *oluolua.* Cool, man cool!"

"Where'd you learn so much about Hawaii and the hula?"

"I had a governess when I was young, in San Francisco. She ta-taught me the da-dance."

Midge was stuttering now in her erotic convulsions. Her head bowed forward, her breasts swung wildly, but her hips kept up that jerking hula movement so swiftly that her rippling flesh seemed almost to blur before my eyes. She began to chant Hawaiian words in tune with her movements until she gasped suddenly and collapsed on me, eyes closed, breathing harshly through her kiss-swollen lips.

"Oh my God," she whimpered after a time. "You're not human."

She fell away from me, sinking onto the cabin floor and resting her flushed cheek on my thigh. After a time she sighed, "I'd do anything for you. Back on the Outer Banks, I knew what I was doing when I tried to keep Laura from killing you."

Her hand pushed her damp blonde hair from her eyes as she stared up at me. "Well? What's the program now?" Her eyes touched the evidence of my priapism, and her red lips smiled faintly. "I can't do anything about that, I'm too tired. You really wear a girl out, you know. So what else do you have in mind?"

"I'm taking you to Bermuda," I said suddenly.

Her eyebrows lifted. "Why Bermuda?"

"There's a friend of mine there I want you to meet."

Bermuda lies roughly eight hundred miles northeast of the Bahamas. In the submersible it would take me forever and a day to reach it, even assuming there was enough fuel in its tank to propel me that far. We had to go back to Grand Bahama and find another way to travel.

After we were clothed—Midge wore my jockey shorts and sports jacket, I was clad in my slacks and shirt—I asked her if she could fly an airplane. She shook her golden hair back and forth, spreading her hands in a helpless gesture.

"So we'll hire a private plane and a pilot," I shrugged.

I have flown planes upon occasion. In an emergency, I could do it again, but I'd feel a lot safer if a regular pilot were sitting at the controls. I put my hands to the controls of the submersible. First things, first. My job right now was to get Midge and myself safely back to shore, then figure out some way of hiding her so Doctor Howard wouldn't find her.

It was close to dawn when I docked the submersible and tied its mooring ropes about the pilings. Midge was hopping up and down on her bare feet to keep warm, making a rather startling picture in my jockey shorts and sports jacket. Since my own chest had only a thin turtleneck over it, I could understand why she felt cold.

Inside the blue Marcos it would be warmer.

We drove to the hotel parking lot. I made Midge give me my sports jacket and left her huddled on the tonneau floor in just my shorts.

"Stay there until I find a friend of mine."

"Female, no doubt?"

"What else? Besides, since you wear female clothes, only a female will be able to supply them."

Redhead was sound asleep when I rang her room. She was grumpy at first but she came alive after I clued her in on the night's events. She promised instant action. She would take Midge a dress and some shoes, and she would hide her in her room. There was a hotel clerk on duty at the registry desk, so my redhead would slip Midge in the back way.

I got into my pajamas and walked around the room smoking cigarettes. I didn't dare sit down on the bed, because I was so pooped I'd have lain back and gone to sleep. And I wanted to be awake when Redhead called.

It seemed an eternity, but the telephone jangled at last. Midge was safe in her room, Redhead told me. She would get a good sleep, she would be undisturbed.

"I need a private plane to fly to Bermuda," I told her.

"The Foundation keeps a Beechcraft Queen Air on call. I'll give her pilot a buzz in the morning, then call you."

I was so tired I forgot to say good-night. I just fell back on the bed and faded into oblivion for about eight hours. My stomach woke me, telling me it needed sustenance.

For once I had no fear of meeting Midge Priest in the hotel dining room. I gorged on flapjacks and sausages, crumb cakes and three cups of hot java. Refreshed by my repast, I went back to my room.

The call came at ten minutes to three.

Redhead told me Midge Priest was at the airport, all set to hop. All I had to do was drive there. The Beechcraft was revving its engines at this very moment.

"Take a taxi," my girl Friday ordered. "That way, the opposition will see the blue Marcos in the hotel parking lot and will think you're up in your room."

That Redhead, she thought of everything.

CHAPTER SEVEN

Walrus-moustache was at the airport to meet us.

As the Beechcraft taxied to a halt on the tarmac at Kindley Field, I could see him sitting upright in a jeep as it sped out to meet us. His right hand was on his hat, he was swathed in a topcoat against the cold wind. His face was set like stone, and it looked unhappy.

His first words fitted his mood, when he saw me.

"You blew it, didn't you?" he asked bitterly.

"Blew it? Don't put me down, Chief. I've got a visitor."

He blinked when I turned back to the Queen Air and told Midge to stir her stumps. She came to the open door and waved a hand at Walrus-moustache. He blinked in disbelief.

"That's the girl who tried to kill Wanda Weaver Yule," he snapped. His eyes swung to me. "What is this?"

"Didn't Redhead tell you? My, my! The girl isn't quite as efficient as I thought. Or maybe she's playing games."

I turned back to the landing ladder to give Midge a hand. The cold wind that was whipping around the field was almost a gale. It blew the mini-skirt Midge was wearing almost to her hips so I got a marvelous view of her leg structure. Midge giggled and fought her skirt and the wind until the chief coughed behind my back.

I introduced them, and added, "Do you mean to say Redhead didn't tell you what happened?"

"I imagine she felt you wanted to tell me yourself. I have a car waiting, so come along."

The Bermudan who drove the little Austin set us down before an old house with a sign in front of it reading:

THE WATERLOT. I gathered it was a place to eat. I was right. It was situated just below the Gibbs Hill lighthouse in a setting that drew a delighted gurgle from Midge Priest.

Inside the Waterlot, under the big cedar beams that ran across the dining room ceiling, Walrus-moustache got down to business. We were alone in the room; the Chief had probably seen to that with a preposterous tip. This was a small room off the main one, which was filled with customers. The waitress even went so far as to close the door behind her when she left, so as to hide us from view, as well as keep our voices unheard.

"Now we can talk," growled the Chief.

I told him everything I'd done since arriving on Grand Bahama island, except for those wild moments in the submersible with Midge. He listened quietly, hunched forward, motioning me to break off my recital only when the waitress knocked on the door.

When I was done, the boss-man turned to the girl. "Is this true? Will you help us nail this Doctor Howard?"

"Of course," Midge said simply. "Rod saved my life; it belongs to him." Her eyes told me something besides her life was mine too, any time I wanted it.

"Well, now. That's fine. It you turn state's evidence, if this case ever comes to trial, I'll see you don't have anything to worry about. So if you'll tell me what you know—never mind what Rod's told me—you tell me."

Over the frog's legs that are very much the specialty of the house at the Waterlot, Midge explained that Howard Hayes Yule had discovered a metallic compound by a form of electrolysis which, when an electric current was shot through it, reacted to the force of gravity.

"I can't explain it any more than that," Midge said apologetically. "I'm not a scientist. All I know is that the heart of the operation is a sealed cylinder set into some sort of ray machine. The cylinder controls the ray process by which the metallic compound is readied for its final use. Once irradiated by the cylinder-ray machine, it becomes capable of reacting to gravity when an electric impulse is shot through it."

99

I asked, "What's to stop Doctor Howard from inspecting the contents of the cylinder and——"

Midge shook her head, interrupting with, "No can do. The cylinder would self-destruct. I've been told that Yule demonstrated this to her when they sat down to talk business. She can make as much of the metallic compound as she wants. She just can't look into that cylinder and know what makes it tick."

"Yule had a built-in safeguard against the double-cross," the Chief nodded. "And then he died." He frowned, thinking for a moment, then added, "I take it this Doctor Howard's a pretty smart scientist?"

"Oh, yes. A very brilliant one. She knew Yule didn't have the time to experiment on this gravity compound which he called Yule-lift but she did. He became partners with her on a venture that would make them both billionaires if it succeeded."

The United States government has been studying gravity for the last twenty years. Teams of scientists are reported to have had varying degrees of success. There is such a thing as a 'spinetic field,' which is said to produce gravitational fields that respond to gravity by adding to or subtracting from the gravitational pull of the Earth.

Any space scientist will tell you that our future in space depends on finding an answer to the force of gravity. The rocket ship we know today is highly inefficient. It must carry most of its weight in fuel. If a working 'spinetic field' could be developed, if a small motor were invented that could create strong spinetic fields to increase the effect of gravity to pull an object toward it, or to decrease gravity to a null-minus effect so gravity would push instead of pull, travel in space would become relatively simple.

The efficient spaceship should be able to use Earth gravity to rise upward away from the planet. There would be no sudden acceleration such as there is now in the Apollo rockets, there would be a gentle acceleration as gravity itself pushed against the space vehicle. On a trip to Mars, say, this gravitational effect would hurl the spacecraft toward the red planet at dizzying speed, once

100

the ship was out in space. As the ship neared Mars, that planet's gravity would take over and attract the ship toward it.

Using the push-pull effect, a landing on a planet could be made softer than that of a parachutist dropping to earth after a leap from a plane. The ship would lower gently, there would be no blasts from rocket jets to disturb the terrain. It would be as if a giant hand were lowering it.

To bring the matter closer to home and this moment in Time, Walrus-moustache pointed out that a nation such as the United States or the Soviet Union could put a space station in the sky without too much trouble, if it possessed this secret of gravitational control. Bands of Yule-lift could be fitted onto the parts of that space station. When an electric current was passed through the Yule-lift, those parts would rise as easily into the air as might a balloon filled with helium gas.

"You can imagine what would happen, then," growled the boss-man. "A space station up there, able to drop atom bombs with pinpoint accuracy, would control the world."

"Yeah," I breathed.

"There would be no more war," the Chief went on. "Everything on Earth would have to submit to the first nation with that space station, if it went that far." He added glumly, "I wouldn't be surprised if scientists came up with some sort of repulsion ray from that Yule-lift compound, so the space station could repel any atomic warheads that might be fired at it."

His fist hit the table. Midge jumped and stifled a scream. Walrus-moustache glowered at both of us. "We have to get that Yule-lift apparatus. Fast!"

Midge spread her hands. "I'd tell you where to find it if I could. I don't know. Only a few technicians whom Beatrice Howard has taken into her confidence know where the Yule-lift lab is."

I frowned. "Howard Yule died a year or two ago. Did this Doctor Beatrice Howard have anything to do with that?"

"No, he died a natural death. He left instructions for

101

Wanda Weaver Yule, his widow, to continue the payments he was making into the Yule-lift project."

"Mmmmm. That's why Doctor Howard wanted Wanda dead, then? To keep her from telling what she knows about the project?"

"Well, no. The reason Doctor Howard wanted Wanda Weaver Yule dead was that Yule's widow wanted to sell her shares of stock in his Yule-lift Corporation. She hasn't the vaguest idea of how valuable those shares are. In her mind, the Yule-lift Corporation is one of her husband's crack-brained ideas. The books show not a penny of profit, so knowing nothing about it, she figured she might as well get rid of a white elephant."

The Chief nodded. "Once she put those shares on the market, any possible buyer would want to look into them, find out about them—and Doctor Howard was going to make sure that didn't happen. When Yule died, she got greedy and decided to keep Yule-lift for herself. Am I right?"

"I'd say it was like that, yes. What Bea hopes to do is put those Yule-lift stocks into an estate, then tie up that estate long enough for her to perfect her gravity experiments and market the final result. The settlement of an estate as large as the Yule one would take at least a couple of years. This would give Doctor Howard plenty of time to complete her experiments."

Midge went on, toying with a bread crumb on the tablecloth, "You see, Howard Hayes Yule realized that his efforts had only scratched the surface of gravity research. His compound would lift little things like a table, a chair, even a child. But he could not go on experimenting himself, so he turned his find over to Bea.

"Doctor Howard has made wonderful strides. As you saw, Rod, we girls can wear a belt of Yule-lift into which we can throw an electric current by turning a small dial on the belt buckle. We can rise up or lower ourselves to the ground without fear. The Yule-lift won't fail us. We all get to practice with it at one time or another."

"I don't understand," the Chief said. "If Wanda Weaver Yule holds the purse-strings, wouldn't Doctor

102

Howard be cutting off her flow of funds by killing her?"

"Oh, no. Yule himself set up a trust fund for the project. Money continues to flow to Doctor Howard, independently of what Wanda Weaver Yule does. The hitch is, the stock is in her name. Wander Weaver Yule is converting a lot of the stock which her husband left her into cash for her mod mod projects—like that school for orphans in New York she built. She's a rich woman, but her supply of funds isn't endless.

"By selling certain stocks, Yule-lift among them, she can get money for her pet charities. Doctor Howard, as I've said, doesn't want any prospective buyer poking around for information. The idea was to gain two years of experimental work by killing Mrs. Yule and tying up her estate.

"Right at this moment Bea is on the verge of making some very important discoveries about Yule-lift. All she needs is time to perfect them. She thinks she knows the inner workings of the cylinder which controls the radiation process. By building a better cylinder, she can improve the performance of the metallic compound. She hopes also that by playing another ultra-high frequency beam through the metallic compound she will add to its power. In other words, her new, improved Yule-lift, when perfected, should be able to lift as heavy an object as a battleship."

"And whammo! The soup hits the electric fan," muttered the Chief. His eyebrows met as he scowled at me. "Damon, it's up to you to stop her."

"Yeah, sure. But how?"

"You tell me. Why should I do all the thinking?"

I pointed out that a number of the girls Doctor Howard employed had seen me and would know me. I could scarcely pretend to be a buyer checking into the stock that Wanda Weaver Yule had offered for sale.

His waving hand brushed this aside. "They're going to know you, anyhow, no matter what part you play."

"True. But I want a fighting chance to stay alive." Walrus-moustache started to speak, but I held up my hand. "Hold it. I'm getting an idea."

The room was very still while I thought. Finally I said,

"Suppose I were to pose as the man who murdered Wanda Weaver Yule?"

Midge exclaimed, "But I shot—I mean, I thought I'd killer her. That's why Doctor Howard was paying me off."

"You told her you killed her," I grinned. "Actually I did the killing—and I want my hundred grand fee."

The Chief frowned. "It might work. At the very least, it would call you to her attention. She might even buy it."

Midge giggled, "It would be a blow below her garterbelt, that's for sure. She might have some use for a hired assassin, at that—somebody who could go out and knock off anybody she wanted dead. But wouldn't she be suspicious? Wouldn't she know you didn't kill Mrs. Yule?"

"You can't tell her, since you'll be here in Bermuda. And how else can she learn the truth?"

The boss-man scowled. "If she learns Wanda Weaver Yule is still alive and kicking—you won't be." His palm hit the tabletop. "I should never have allowed her to go to that orphan school ceremony."

"It poses a bit of a problem, but I can lie my way out of it. I can always say I only wounded her, that she's still alive—and needs killing again. The worst thing that can happen then is, I won't get my hundred grand fee."

"How will you say Midge hired you?"

I shrugged. "I knew Midge in—say, San Francisco. She knew I was a small-time mobster in need of cash. At the last moment, her nerve failed her, so she asked me to do the job. She saw a way to collect the money for herself, she double-crossed me and flew down here to collect ahead of me. I was laying low for a while to let the murder blow over. It might even be a good move on my part to tell her Wanda is still alive."

Midge shivered, reaching out to put a hand on mine. "You be careful, Rod. Beatrice Howard isn't playing games. She's a tough cookie. She might have you killed and check your story later. When you mention my name, you're going to raise her hackles. She's going to be damn suspicious. She may play along with you—only to set you up for the kill."

"I've thought of that," I admitted glumly.

The boss-man announced cheerfully, "Every one of his assignments are setups for Rod to get killed. The professor is used to it."

Big help, the Chief.

Midge murmured, "Maybe you ought to stay on in Bermuda for a few days, to rest up and relax your nerves. Then when you go back to the Bahamas, you'll be in better shape."

Walrus-moustache said briskly, ignoring Midge, "Your plane ought to be refueled by this time, Professor. It will take you back to Freeport airfield in time for you to have dinner with Doctor Howard."

Midge drooped. She brightened when we were walking out into the Bermuda sunshine, Walrus-moustache had fallen behind to pay the tab. Her hand caught mine and pressed it.

"Hurry back, Rod. The two samples of your priapism that you've given me have really interested me in your case. I think another test is called for. I'm still not sure you're what you say you are." She sighed, adding, "And for goodness sake, take care of yourself."

I was very determined to take care of myself. In the Beechcraft Queen Air, as it flew over the Atlantic toward Grand Bahama island, I went over my coming meeting with Doctor Beatrice Howard. Midge was right. She would be damn suspicious of anyone phoning her and mentioning the name of the girl her organization had tried to kill. Come to think of it, those girl guards I'd battled on the *Albatross* deck might recognize me. Then there would be hell to pay, for sure.

There was somebody else who knew I was no hired killer. Laura Ogden. I just hoped that her duties kept her as far away from me as possible. Otherwise—well, I refused to think about what might happen if Laura saw me.

I telephoned Doctor Beatrice Howard as soon as I was in my hotel room. Midge had given me her number, explaining that she rented a little house along the shore of Bell Bay, where she came to relax from time to time. She would be there now, she had told Midge on the *Albatross* she was going there for a few days. She was out.

Next morning, I called up Doctor Beatrice Howard again.

Her voice was softly curious when she answered my ring. "Hello? Who is this?" she asked.

"You don't know me, Doctor Howard," I said, "unless Midge Priest told you about me. My name is Rod Damon."

There was a silence. Then: "I'm afraid Midge has been reticent, Mr. Damon. I don't know you from Adam, and I don't think I care to."

"One hundred thousand, Doctor," I said quickly, afraid she might hang up. "Those are the number of reasons you should know me."

"Oh?"

"Dollars, you might say," I chipped in.

"Ahh. One hundred thousand dollars. What have I to do with them?"

"You owe them to me, for a job well done."

Again that silence touched the other end of the line. "I believe I'd like an explanation, if you don't mind," she murmured at last.

"Naturally. Would you care to join me for dinner this evening? My treat, of course. I'm most anxious to meet you. Midge has spoken so highly of—your organization."

"Why not come out here now, for a drink? I never make blind dates for dinner. Oh—and bring your bathing suit. The day is hot, the sea is smooth. You might like to take a dip."

My last dip, with your girl scuba divers waiting underneath the surface to drown me? Uh-uh, Doctor Howard. But I might wear a bathing suit, at that.

"Be glad to," I said out loud. "Sounds like fun."

The blue Marcos 1600 purred beautifully all the way to Bell Bay. I braked in front of a small white house with brilliant yellow shutters, yellow roof and a white picket fence running alongside the road that enclosed a flagstone-walked garden. As I opened the garden gate, I caught a glimpse of a sandy shore beyond it, and the green waters of Bell Bay glinting in the sunshine.

106

My finger pressed the doorbell.

I did not know what to expect as I stood there. Would somebody holding a gun appear, and would the gun fire at at me as soon as the door opened? I doubted anything as drastic would happen. Doctor Howard was no fool; she would want to find out how much I knew about her organization and whether I had left any documents—in case an accident happened to me—that might lead to her doorstep.

The door swung inward.

I guess I goggled, just a little. Beatrice Howard was standing there clad in a Riviera bikini, than which there is nothing smaller. She had a body that would have tempted an Anthony, if he could have seen it. Her breasts were big white bulges scarcely hidden behind the tiny cups of her halter. Her belly was a mound of sleek flesh, bared down to her privacy where the other part of the bikini was supposed to cover her. She didn't look like a high school physics teacher any more. She appeared to have lost all her prudishness.

Her eyes were heavily lidded as she stared at me. "Mr. Damon? Come in, come in. I'm dying of the heat, so please excuse my informal attire."

"I wouldn't have it any other way," I smiled, stepping through the doorway.

I was half expecting a couple of those girls in the black satin uniforms to come bounding out of the woodwork, their guns blazing. Except for Beatrice Howard and myself, the house was empty, apparently.

She walked ahead of me, showing off her handsome legs and the lower halves of her buttocks to my gaze. Thin straps held her bikini bottoms to her tanned hips. She was all woman, this one. Funny, I'd had her figured all wrong.

There was a cocktail shaker on the buffet. "Daiquiri?" she asked, turning slightly, with a faint smile. "I pride myself on my daiquiries. I think you'll like them."

Were they poisoned? I wondered. I said, "Love one, or maybe even a couple. You're right, it is a hot day. It's about time we got some nice weather."

She brought my drink to me, her hips swaying lazily,

107

her breasts bobbing almost out of their cups. She smiled when she noticed where I was looking. Well, she had nothing to be ashamed of in the body department.

"Cheers," I said, lifting my glass.

I waited until she drank before I put the glass to my mouth. There was nothing wrong with her drink either. It was nectar laced with rum.

"Did you wear a bathing suit?" she wondered.

"Under my slacks."

"Then let's go out into the sun. I've been neglecting my tan. I've been so busy I haven't had time for the fun things of life." She put her empty glass on the buffet, giving me a sidelong glance. She asked, "Now what's this all about?"

"Are we alone? I don't like blabbing in front of witnesses. Maybe we ought to go out on the beach before I start yakking."

She smiled fainlty, nodding. "Yes. I like caution in a man with something to hide. Even though I am alone with you."

I took off my jacket. "Shall I go upstairs to undress?"

"You can put your things over a chair here. But suit yourself."

Her eyes watched as I unbuttoned my shirt and yanked it off to show my tanned, somewhat hairy chest. I unbuckled my belt, slid down my slacks. I was wearing a pair of white nylon swim trunks. They made me look even more tanned, more rugged, than I normally do.

Interest was in her eyes, all right. I am not the founder of the League for Sexual Dynamics for nothing. I know when a woman is wanting, the way she looks at a man. Beatrice Howard was in heat, even though she probably didn't realize it. Few women take the trouble to analyze their emotions, their feminine mystique.

I did, because it was my livelihood.

"I have towels," she told me, "so let's go."

I padded after her quivering behind out the back door and down a row of flaggings to the beach. She walked with a sway of her hips that I knew was unintentional. Doctor Howard was no tease; she considered herself above things like that, I am sure. She didn't know that she was making

108

her curving hips sway and her buttocks jiggle; it was an entirely subconscious movement.

On the beach, I walked beside her to a big maroon beach towel spread out on the sand. She sat down gracefully, making room on the blanket for me.

"There's nobody around, as you can see for yourself," murmured the woman, "so why not tell me why I owe you a hundred thousand dollars?"

"I killed a woman for you."

Her eyes widened slightly. "Did you?"

"Well, I shot her. Unfortunately, she was wearing a kind of protective vest and I didn't do much more than wound her."

"What's that?" she rasped, sitting up and staring at me.

I smiled at her. "I can always do it again. Relax. So you wanted Wanda Weaver Yule dead and Midge couldn't do it. I stepped in and pulled the trigger."

She was damn near choking. "I don't know what you're talking about!"

"Sure you do, honey. The Yule woman, remember? Her husband was your partner in some sort of scientific experiment before he died. Midge told me a little about it. Where is Midge, by the way?"

Beatrice Howard was torn between fear and fury. She tried to speak three times before she could twist her tongue around a few syllables. "Midge is—on a job," she managed to say.

"Good for her. She tried to do the job, you know—kill that Yule dame, I mean—but she just doesn't have the killer instinct. I had to do it for her. She promised you'd pay me a hundred thousand for it. I'm here to collect."

"I—paid—Midge," she snarled.

"You're putting me on," I exclaimed in seeming disbelief.

"I'm not in the habit of telling lies, Mr. Damon!"

I lifted my hands, palms toward her, placatingly. "Take it easy. Don't get mad. If Midge is trying to do me one, I'll take care of the matter myself." I hesitated, then said, "The trouble is, our victim is still alive, I'm afraid. Midge beat it before we were sure. I guess she wanted to collect

109

that fee and lose herself. But she won't get away from me."

Doctor Howard had calmed down a little by this time. Her slim black brows rose inquiringly. "She won't get away? She has gotten away. Some scuba diver rescued her from—"

I laughed and slapped my thigh. "Is that how you play the game, doctor? Give your killers the payoff—then kill them? Naughty, naughty. I don't like dishonest people."

She never turned a hair. "Midge was untrustworthy. You yourself told me she blabbed what she knew about me and—and my experiments."

"You didn't know that when you tried to get rid of her."

Her hand went down to the sand, which she began sifting through her fingers. "How much did she tell you about my work?"

"You kidding? How do you think I was able to shoot Wanda Weaver Yule through the window of her hotel suite thirty stories above the ground, unless I was wearing one of those gravity belts?"

Her eyes ran over my muscular body. "It shouldn't have worked with you. It wasn't strong enough."

"It was a mite slow getting me back to my own room in the Waldorf. But it did the job. Oh, I tested it beforehand, to be on the safe side."

Her eyes were very direct. "Even granting all that, what do you want from me now? You said yourself this Wanda Weaver Yule is still alive."

"Yeah, she is. And she's being damn well guarded by a bunch of smart cookies. It won't be as easy to do her in next time."

"But you have an idea?"

"Right the first time. I'm going to kill her in a way that will look like an accident. Don't worry. You can leave it to me. If you're still interested in her death, that is."

"I am. I admit it."

"Tell you what, Doctor. I'll throw in Midge Priest for the price of killing the Yule woman. How does that strike you? Not only will I kill Midge, but I'll turn over the

110

money Midge stole from you by telling you those lies."

"How come? You don't strike me as the generous type."

I studied the way her breasts bulged into nakedness above her scanty bikini cups, at the slightly pouching belly above the tiny triangle of nylon hiding her *mons veneris*. I smiled into her black eyes.

"You need a man, Doctor."

She flushed, and her eyes flickered. "I consider that an insult," she breathed, and started to get to her feet.

I reached out, caught her arm, drew her bouncing back onto the beach towel. She landed with a thump on her soft rump and her breasts jumped clear out of the nylon cups. Her brown nipples were thickly swollen. She gave a little cry and tried to cover those big white mounds with her palms.

"You need a man that way, too, honey—but what I was referring to was a man to do your dirty jobs. You know, like killing Wanda Weaver Yule and Midge Priest. Like protecting you if anybody sticks his nose into your affairs the way I'm doing right now."

"You bastard!" she whispered.

"Sure, sure. But you need me. You know you do. A woman can't go it alone in this world of ours without a tough man to side her. Midge said you employed very few men, and those are mostly all the brainy types. You don't have a hard-hitter in the bunch. And, lady, you really need a hard-hitter."

Her red mouth sneered at me. "I suppose you think you're tough! You're nothing but a windbag. Filled with hot air. Now get out of my sight."

"You aren't thinking, lady. I know too much, but I wouldn't run to the fuzz. I have bigger plans than that."

She had her hands up in front of her breasts, replacing the nylon cups. She was breathing harshly, making her task a difficult one because her breasts kept jumping up and down, in and out of the cups.

"What sort of plans?" she panted.

"Plans that include you as the boss. I couldn't carry out your experiments, you ought to know that. I'm just your

111

insurance against trouble. Your partner, let's say."

"You're just nothing," she snapped. Her head tilted to one side as she sneered, "I don't think you're tough enough to be my partner."

She rose to her feet, one grand specimen of a female, almost naked in the Bahaman sunlight. "Let's go get cool. Then we can talk about how tough you are."

Her back was soft between the thongs of her bikini top and the straps of her bottom, as she turned away from me and began walking toward the sea. I got up and went after her, following her dive into the cold water.

She swam well, quite strongly for a woman. Once she turned her head and called, "Race you to the buoy!" I guess she figured she would be testing my toughness that way.

The buoy was a hundred yards out. I passed her in fifteen strokes and built a big lead into twenty full yards by the time she reached the black and white marker. I was hanging to it with a hand when she came stroking up, so I reached out to catch her and bring her closer.

Her soft body bumped into my male strength.

She tried to push free, but my arm around her waist held her right there in front of me. Her face was wet and her eyes were stormy.

"Let me go, damn you! I'm not one of your floozies."

I tightened my hold, making sure her loins rubbed mine while her breasts mashed on my chest. I grinned down at her. "Honey, you're going to be mine. You don't realize it, but you're dying to wrap your legs about my hips and start playing."

She tried to slap me, but I held her arms tight against her sides so she could only pant and wriggle in my embrace. "I'll kill you, I swear to God I'll put a bullet in you!"

"Go on—fight. I like a girl who doesn't know what she wants. She's always so grateful when I show her."

She snarled at me, but she did not struggle any more. She let her softness move against my hardness to the lift and swell of the waves, she stared coldly past my left

112

shoulder as her waist gave to my arm that held her against me.

"This is the cold shoulder treatment." I smiled down into her angry face. "I can always predict it."

"Can you also predict what will happen to you when I get my hands on a gun?"

"You won't shoot. You're enjoying this too much."

I let her go after a time. We couldn't stay out here like this forever. She turned and swam away without a single glance at me. I began to worry that I'd overplayed my hand. The worry was with me all the way back to the beach.

Beatrice Howard stalked up the sand and toward her house. Not feeling like sitting out in the sun as a target for gunfire, I trailed her jiggling behind into the house. She walked to the buffet table and opened a drawer. She reached into it.

Her hand lifted out a Colt revolver, .32 calibre.

A .32 can kill a man just as dead as a .45. She looked at me with the gun in her steady hand and sneered, "You're so tough. Beg me not to shoot you. Let's see how really tough you are, buster."

I was maybe ten feet away. I spread my hands and smiled at her. "You won't shoot me, honey. You're still too curious about me. Dead, I can't tell you what you want to know—like how come I know Midge Priest and whether I've left any papers that will incriminate you and your organization in case you shoot me dead."

I was moving forward slowly as I talked, waving my hands for greater emphasis. She was looking me right in the eye; somebody probably told her at one time that you can see a warning signal in your opponent's eye before he makes a move against you.

You can, of course. But not if he guards against it. My eyes were calm and untroubled as I went on arguing. My hands talked for me, too, waving around like signal flags.

I got her used to my hands flapping like that, so she paid them no nevermind. When I got close to her I let her have my left hand across the inside of her wrist, taking her

113

by surprise. The gun flew wide. My right hand swung, grabbed her gun-hand and held on. She fought, her bare foot thudding into my ankle. She scratched my arm and bent her head to try and bite me.

I hit her wrist against the edge of the buffet.

She cried out in pain and let go of the gun. I kicked it across the room with a bare foot. I was jammed up into her soft female body with my loins flat against her loins. I let myself rub against her there until she felt the telltale bulge in my swimsuit that told her I was more man than enemy.

"I'm going to show you how tough I am," I smiled.

"Go to hell!"

"Tsk, tsk, for shame."

I held her pressed back into the buffet with the front of my body. My hands bent her arms around behind her so I could catch her wrists in the fingers of my left hand and hold them. She fought fiercely to get free but when I jammed my loins into her, driving her wrists back into the buffet, she lost a little of her truculence.

"Admit it, honey," I wheedled. "You want loving."

Her reply was unprintable. I bent and kissed her soft throat, making sure my earlobe was out of reach of her white teeth. She snarled and struggled, but my strength was a little too much for her.

With my teeth, I got a grip on the nylon cup that shielded the nipple of her left breast. I tugged and the cup came away, her breast bulging outward over its wired rim. I caressed the nipple with my tongue, lazily, tauntingly.

"Stop," she wailed. "Please, stop!"

"I know you better than you know yourself, Doctor," I whispered into her swollen breastflesh. "You're going to thank me for this, a little later."

She sobbed above my head as I paid lip service to her nipple. The female breast is a mass of nerves that respond with erotic eagerness to kisses and tongue-bathings. The nipple will swell from one to one and a half centimeters, and will increase its diameter at the base from one-half to one centimeter. The areolas, that broad circle of color about the nipples, will puff up, engorging with blood. The

114

breast itself will swell from a fifth to one quarter more than its normal size.

Beatrice Howard was no exception to the rule. Her nipples were damn near an inch long in their excited condition, and her breasts had grown bloated, hard as marble. She was moaning low in her throat, turning her flushed face from side to side.

I whispered to her saliva-wet nipple, "Promise to be a good girl?"

She nodded, muttering, "Yes, just let me go."

I released her wrists, stepped back.

She brought her hands out from behind her and leaped for me, fingers curved like claws. I half expected this. I dodged. I slapped the back of my hand against her left cheek. She let out a yell and flew sideways, banging into the dining room wall.

I gave her no chance to get her breath. I stepped behind her, catching both her wrists and bending them up behind her almost naked back.

"So," I breathed into her ear. "You can be trusted about as far as I can throw an elephant. Well, it fits in with what Midge said about you. What did you plan to do with Midge, anyhow? Kill her? And then take back your hundred grand? I wouldn't put it past you."

She was choking and sputtering in the sheer violence of her rage. She tried to kick back with her heels at my shins. I bent both her arms up behind her back while her forehead was pressed into the wall. She screamed.

"I don't think I want you as a partner, after all," I told her pink ear under its spill of long black hair. "I wouldn't have a minute's peace with you, not knowing how and when you were going to cheat me."

She was quivering, weeping silently. My manhood was pressed into her soft, bulging buttocks. I nudged her there in a gentle side-to-side rhythm. She felt how aroused I had become. Unless my senses were deceiving me, she was returning my pressure, rubbing back against me with her all but naked behind.

I am certain she would have denied it, but the fact was irrefutable. Her body was betraying her mind, proof

115

positive that I was absolutely right about Doctor Beatrice Howard. She wanted it, but bad.

"You're only good for one thing," I snapped. "You figure out what it is."

I held both her wrists with my left hand. With my right, I unfastened her halter. Her heavy breasts fell into view, reflected in the buffet mirror. The brown nipples were swollen, enlarged.

With my free hand, I toyed with those breasts, tugging and pulling on the stiffened nipples, caressing the sleek skin with my palm. I whispered little love words into her ear, and paused from time to time to bite her soft throat.

I was getting to her, there was no doubt about that, but she still wanted to fight. Some women are like that. They have a guilt feeling about sex and like a man to take the decision out of their hands. They have to be raped to enjoy it, then they have the excuse to salve their consciences.

So I clawed at her bikini bottoms, tearing the thin straps in getting them off her hips. She was naked now, bent before me, sobbing deep in her throat.

I let her go, shoving her forward. She slipped and fell to the floor on her hands and knees. I freed my loins of my swimsuit.

Beatrice Howard was not moving; she still posed like that, with her palms flat on the carpet, knees pressing into the rug. There seemed to be an acceptance of the inevitable in her flesh. Until I dropped on her from behind, that is.

"No!" she screamed thickly, diving to one side. "No, goddam you! I say you won't get anything out of me."

She slid sideways, turning to drive a bare foot at my manhood. I took the foot on my thigh. I caught the hands that clawed at my face. I let my weight drop on her naked body. The wind whooshed out of her lungs. She writhed sideways, head going back and forth.

Her lips spewed profanity, backdrawn to expose her teeth.

I used my weight and my muscles to flatten her spine on the rug as my hand went to her soft thighs, forcing her

116

to widen them. All this time I stared down into her blazing eyes. There were no tears in those eyes; she was not weeping. Instead, there was a red rage defying me to overcome her. If I was to enjoy her body, I must conquer her flesh.

"You want to know how tough I am?" I grinned down into her snarling features. "I'm tough enough to rape you and make you like it."

"You never could!" she sobbed.

"Watch and see, Doctor. I have no pity for a dame like you, who doesn't know she's burning up for a man. But maybe you're the best kind, after all. You're so eager for it, you can hardly wait."

I stared down between her wide white thighs. She was ready for me, all right. Her business end was literally swimming. Doctor Howard moaned, half in shame, half in sheer want. Her tanned thighs were yawning in welcome, she had not the will nor the strength to close them.

I slid forward into place, laughing softly.

Forgotten were the niceties of love-making. This woman wanted no part of them, she wanted only the brutal taking, the escape from guilt, the decision taken out of her hands. I drove into her.

Her head rocked back, her throat strutted with the unvoiced cry of delight. She was no virgin, but she was no roundheels either. It had been a long time for Beatrice Howard but her glands had been on my side, even if her brain and will were not. She was moist, ready as any female to take a man. She and her struggles were liars.

When I was deep within her flesh, she abandoned those struggles. Her arms and her legs embraced me. She gyrated and swung beneath me like a machine, panting out words in my ear.

"Damn you for doing this to me! Damn you! I thought I'd gotten beyond this sort of thing. You raped me, damn you for a bastard! You raped me. You didn't get me to accept this sort of thing."

"You want me to stop?" I asked brutally.

Her arms and legs tightened. Against my chest her breasts were big white rocks, solid marble in her rut. She moaned. "No, no, no. Don't stop. Please don't stop. You

117

don't know how many nights I've lain awake dreaming about something like this. In my laboratories I'm a coldly reasoning scientist but sometimes when the sun goes down I ache from the need for this.

"I walk my bedroom floor; I tell myself I'm a slut, an easy lay, that I'm no better than a whore. Well, goddamnit, I can't help it. Do you dig me, man? I just can't help myself."

Her hips were rocking me back and forth and from side to side. Beatrice Howard was living out her nighttime fantasies with my body. I might as well be headless and speechless, as far as she was concerned. To her I was an amorous automaton, no more. And then resentment to this anonymity began to build in me.

I had to make her acknowledge my existence as Rod Damon. I was not indulging her flesh cravings out of pure lust. I was working as a Coxeman right now, to build a realization in Doctor Howard that I was her man, her tough boy to side her against the outside world. I had to make her understand that without me she was nothing, that she had to have me by her side all the time.

So I caught her hips and forced her back away from me.

She lay like the mother of all whores, thighs spread wide, gasping and panting for a male. I grinned down at her horrified expression.

"What? Why did you stop? Oh, God—please!"

"Remember me, honey? I'm Rod Damon. The tough guy who is going to kill your enemies for you."

"Come on, come in!"

Her pallid hips lifted and swung. She was mindless, living only in her femininity. I felt pity for her. I do not enjoy being cruel to a wanting woman. But I was playing for greater stakes than a quick lay. I was trying to build a place for me in her life.

I leaned forward and downward, I commenced the *tekhfidz* play of male member with female organ, that lazy caress of one with the other on the labia major, which is known also as rubbing the pencil in the kohl pot. The

118

Turks call this movement 'whitewashing'—*bedana*—because the penis resembles the brush coating the walls to be painted.

It is a movement exacerbating to the female, it teases her to madness. It is mentioned in the laws of Islam, the El-Hhidayeh, as a crime—unless the male gives the female the full penetration of his organ within hers.

She was weeping real tears, her flushed face distorted as her head went back and forth. Her body was trying to catch me, to trap me to her enjoyment, but I am not the founder of the League for Sexual Dynamics for nothing. This was my thing. I had the opportunity of stamping this woman with the badge of my manhood, to reduce her to an animal dependency on me. I was not about to give up that advantage until she became what I wanted her to become.

Beatrice Howard seemed to sense this, for after several minutes of sobbed curses and vain strivings to unite herself with me, she became almost calm as she looked up at my naked body.

"What do you want?" she breathed.

"I want you as a woman, not a mare, unthinking and ungrateful," I told her. "My name is Rod Damon, I'm a killer for hire. You and I will make sweet music if you come to your senses."

Tears welled up in her eyes. "I c-can't help it. It's been so long. Please! Please—Rod!"

"Ahhh, that's better," I nodded, lowering my body.

I let her have what she wanted for long minutes, until her body had contracted in the orgasmal spasm half a dozen times. I blunted the sharp edge of her want with the *tachik el heub* movements that pounded me into her flesh. This particular motion is known as the capturing of love, since it involves a penetration of the entire length of the male within the female. The resultant movement of the male results in utter ecstasy for the woman.

She was almost in a coma when I moved away to find a damp cloth and dry her face and body. She smiled as I tended her—she did not expect tenderness after rape. I

119

soothed her with my voice, telling her she and I were not yet done, that we would be partners in all things, even this.

When life came back into her body, she looked up at me wonderingly. Her interest centered on the fact that my flesh was as ready for love as it had been before I had entered her. She looked so naive that I bent and kissed her gently.

"Don't mind me. I suffer from priapism," I told her.

I explained a little about priapism until she nodded her acceptance of the fact. Her bare arms came up about my neck. "I'll have to do something about it. I think I can, when I get my breath."

She got her breath back pretty damn fast because she slithered her nakedness against my front, dragging her big breasts along my torso from my pectoral muscles to my upper thighs, back and forth and across. She gurgled laughter when she saw how aroused my flesh became when her nipples caressed it.

Beatrice Howard came to her hands and knees, pushed me back so I lay flat on the carpet. She dragged her dangling breasts up and down my nakedness. She seemed to get a charge out of the fact that she could tease me so exquisitely with her mammaries.

Doctor Howard apparently had decided to make the most of what she was being given. She was exclaiming her own enjoyment of her acts, as if her wriggling hips weren't tip-off enough to my trained eyes.

Before long, she was sobbing in sheer rut.

"Do me, do me, do me," she kept moaning.

Her head lowered to below my abdomen. Her wet lips were generous with kisses and bites. I started to sob myself. I may have had to rape Beatrice Howard, but once she got turned on and tuned in, she was a regular Jezebel. Her harsh breathing filled the air. Her eyes were closed, her mouth was necessarily a little open as her head bobbed up and down.

When I figured she was close to hysteria, I slid out from under her and around behind her. The manner of the cow, as mentioned by Vatsyayana, is highly recommended by

120

the Hindu erotologists because the accompanying caresses that should attend this intimate act can be carried on by the man with both hands free.

He is able to clasp and fondle the female breasts and nipples, to play at games with them. He may stroke the belly in rhythm to his hip motions, he may even add his fingers to the caressing strokes of his lingam within the female yoni.

I did all these things and more to Beatrice Howard.

Her backside twisted and wriggled as she drove herself along with me, crying out her pleasure from moment to moment. She was a mare with a stallion, a cow with a bull, a bitch with a hound as her buttocks swung and looped and shook. Her hanging head was bent as if in submission to the fleshy storm racking her body. She was alive only in her starved femininity.

And because mine was the lingam that afforded her this *nayf*, or pleasure of the flesh, she became eternally grateful to me. She whispered words that told me this, though they were half unintelligible, and her hanging hair as it brushed the floor was a steady whisper of praise for my erotic efforts.

Beatrice Howard tried, but she could not match my priapism. At length she begged me to stop, that she was too worn out, too sore to continue. I was the master and she the slave, she admitted, but she pleaded with me to show my slave some mercy.

I pulled free of her clasp and watched as she collapsed limply to the carpet. I bent and kissed her spine all the way to the cleavage of her buttocks. Then I turned her over and kissed from her pubic hair upward to her moist red mouth. She moaned faintly and let her hand touch my head.

"I'll carry you to bed," I breathed.

I got my arms under her knees and shoulders and lifted her. She was a big woman, but I am a strong man. I made it up the stairs without any trouble.

She seemed almost like a little girl as I pulled the coverlets up beneath her chin. Her eyes were big and her lips drooped a little. "You aren't going away, are you? I mean,

121

you'll stay for the night? There's food downstairs, plenty of it."

I sat on the edge of the bed, nodding. "Of course I'll stay. You need a man around the house, honey—and not just to make sure you get rid of your enemies."

She nodded. The hardness had been washed out of her, she was a female with a man who could please her body to such an extent that this was all she wanted to know about him. Beatrice Howard had been on a sex starvation diet for a long time. Now she was seeing herself catered to in every way by a man who knew how to thrill her senses.

"I'll fix a tray with some food," I told her, patting her hand. "You sleep for a while. I'll wake you when it's time to eat."

She slept like a baby.

I folded my frame on a couch in her living room after pulling down the blinds, so I would be rested for the evening activities. My campaign to make a slave of Doctor Beatrice Howard was just beginning.

CHAPTER EIGHT

The sun was hot, the water was green, the air was scented with the blend of salt and Joy perfume as the big Chris-Craft skimmed the waves of Nurse Channel in the Exuma Cay sector of the Bahama islands. We were moving past Ragged Island Cays at a good clip; Bea was at the wheel and I was close beside her, enjoying the sun, the air, and her nearness.

We had flown from Great Bahama Island to Nassau on New Providence island, then to Clarence Town on Long Island, where the Chris-Craft had been lodged. Three days ago I had met Doctor Howard for the first time; today she was like a new woman.

"We have a big Quonset hut on Gabber Cay," she cried against the wind whipping past the curving glass shield. "That's where we test my findings."

"You're being mysterious about it," I accused.

She turned her head to blow a kiss at me. Beatrice Howard was a changed woman. Gone was the prude, the modest dress, the air of dedicated scientist. During those two days we had spent together in her little house Bea had thrown herself with no reservations into the sexual frenzies I had devised for her complete subjection to my manhood.

No longer was she Puritan in dress. Witness: she wore the bikini in which her all but naked body had greeted me at her house. She told me it was the first time she had worn it, to see what manner of man I was, to test that manhood and laugh at me when she threw me aside. Instead, I had made her my slave. Normally, she wore a very

123

modest, almost matronly bathing suit, she informed me.

But now—

The tiny cups of her bikini halter, the thin straps and twin triangles about her loins, were all she was wearing. "My body feels new—alive. Freer than it's ever been. And you've caused that change in me, Rod."

The little island hove into view off our port bow, low in the water, not much more than a small coral isle with some sand dunes, a few rocks, and a few bushes growing on its few inches of dirt. The Quonset hut made a big bump almost in its exact middle.

"I needed seclusion to make my tests, and the hut was the best way to do it. I bought it in a sale of old war surplus materials and had it shipped down here."

"You must be pretty rich," I pointed out.

"I make do with what I have. I'll be even richer, a lot richer, Rod, when I succeed in my experiments. And so will you."

She said nothing about Howard Hayes Yule and his widow, Wanda. She wanted me to think her own money was backing her project. This was fine with me, because I wasn't telling her that I planned to bring her project down around her ears like a house of cards collapsing.

A small quay of thin saplings with heavier pilings loomed before us as she swung the wheel to nose the Chris-Craft in against the wooden poles. I sprang to the foredeck, reached for a rope, flung it over a piling.

To my surprise, Beatrice Howard was tugging off her bikini halter, baring her breasts to the Bahaman sunlight. She giggled, catching my interested stare.

"I can't walk in on—them—like this," she protested, bending forward to search in her little carrying case for a black brassiere. She lifted it up, letting her breasts slip into the cups. Almost breathlessly, she added, "They think I'm a dedicated scientist."

Her chin lifted defiantly. "Well, I am. But I guess I'm also a woman, even if I have fought against it." She found a sweater in her case and slipped it on over her upper body.

Her fingers were busy with her bikini bottom straps.

124

She untied them, tossed the thin triangles aside. Naked below her sweater, her pallid hips and buttocks shining whitely in the sunlight, she flushed faintly.

"Aren't you worried about them seeing you?" I asked.

She shook her head, bringing a garterbelt out of her small valise and hooking it about her middle. "They're all busy working. I have a good organization, darling. They go on working whether I'm here or not."

Over the garterbelt she pulled on a pair of nearly transparent black nylon panties. Then she sat down on a motorboat seat and, extending a slim leg, began drawing on a sheer nylon stocking. Her thigh turned sideways as she bent her head to watch as her fingers gartered the stocking vamp.

Within moments she was twisting into a skirt, standing now, half laughing as she caught my eyes. "There, I'm the lady boss once more. Nobody will know the way I've been showing off my body almost naked—except you. And you have the right to see me like that, Rod."

She slipped her feet into high-heeled shoes and reached up her hand for me to take. I helped steady her as she stepped from the Chris-Craft onto the quay. As she walked ahead of me toward the shore, she showed a pair of handsome legs between her high heels and high skirt.

In a way, it was a damn shame to blow the whistle on Doctor Beatrice Howard. Under different circumstances, she could have been much fun.

I went after her stockinged legs up a stone path to a big flagstoned patio that held some outdoor furniture and then along a walkway that twisted upward and straightened to run toward the Quonset hut.

"This is testing day," she said, walking side by side with me along the wide path. "My whole gang will be here to make notes, to plan revisions, to see how experimental ideas have come out in the test run."

I heard voices and some laughter as her hand pushed open the door. A man stood there, uniformed like a private policeman, a Colt .45 hanging in a black leather holster at his hip. He touched the peak of his cap when he saw Bea, and gave me a sharp look out of pale blue eyes.

His face was tough, leathery; I told myself to be careful of this one, he was the kind who shot first, then thought about asking questions.

We went through a kind of crude lobby with a big door straight ahead and a smaller door off to one side, and stepped into a vast hall with a curving ceiling painted in sky blue and white fluff to represent clouds. It made the entire scene appear to be outdoors in the fresh air. Hidden lights, air vents and the painted ceiling made everything look realistic.

There were about a dozen girls and eight or nine young men, inside the hut. Ten of the girls and four of the young men were in the air, rising and falling like living elevators, as four of the men and two of the girls—all of them clad in white lab smocks—stared up at them and made notes on pieces of paper attached to clipboards.

One of the men turned his head, saw Bea, and put a whistle to his mouth. The sound rang through the hut. At that signal, the girls moving up and down in their gravity belts touched their controls and lowered to the hard dirt floor.

Doctor Howard said, "I want you to meet Rod Damon. He's going to be my partner from now on. There are to be no secrets from him."

I searched their faces, hunting for that of Laura Ogden. She was the one weak link in my chain of sabotage. I could never persuade her that I was not the Coxeman she believed me to be when she'd left me to die in the cellar of the Outer Banks house.

There was no Laura Ogden. Instead, I saw eager young faces, heard the murmur of soft voices. The girls were all slimly supple, good-looking, and very sexy. Maybe they looked so sexy because they were so healthy. They crowded in around me with questions babbling on their lips.

Doctor Howard raised her arms. "Quiet, quiet. You'll get to meet him socially later. Right now I want you to show him that our Space Travel Limited gravity belts really work."

The girls who had been testing the belts were wearing

126

tight body-stockings, some of sheer black nylon, some of red lace, some of blue or white or pink rayon. Under those form-tight suits their bodies were naked. When they jumped around in their enthusiasm, their breasts shook and bobbled.

Their sexiness gave me an idea.

My job was to find out where Space Travel Ltd. had its laboratories, so the Coxe Foundation could destroy them. I told myself there was nothing to help me inside the Quonset hut, but in the outer lobby where the armed guard was, I had seen a closed door. Reason told me that Doctor Howard would have an office inside the hut, to file away reports on the tests she took. Where those reports were kept, I might find some hint of where the laboratories themselves could be located.

I said, "I'd like to try a belt myself."

One of the young men in the white smocks turned to a table and lifted a belt, handing it to me. I strapped it about my middle.

Remembering that I had told Doctor Howard I had worn such a belt when I shot Wanda Weaver Yule, I said, "I know a little about them, but you'd better explain their workings to refresh my memory."

He showed me the little dial on the belt buckle. To put power into the belt to lift it, I simply turned the dial. It sent an electric current through the belt, which was fashioned of leather into which the metallic compound called Yule-lift had been stitched. This would lift me upward. When I wanted to come down I would simply cut down on the amount of electric current I was feeding into the belt.

I turned the dial.

Nothing happened.

Everybody started to talk, crowding in around me. Doctor Howard pushed forward, nodding her head. "Just as I thought. The belt isn't strong enough yet to lift a man as large as you."

She glanced at me suspiciously, frowning. I knew what was in her mind. She was wondering how in hell I had used Midge's belt to shoot Wanda Weaver Yule. I winked

127

at her, grinned happily, and she seemed to relax. I told myself to think fast; I needed a damn good explanation to cover up for my goof.

A man brought another belt and I buckled it about my middle. This time when I pressed the two buckle-dials, I shot up into the air.

"Woowww!" I yelled.

"Not so much juice," a girl called.

She apparently thought I needed help because she turned her own dials and rose up into the air after me. I stared down at the red hair framing her upturned face. She was laughing delightedly at my predicament. There was no danger, her blue eyes were telling me as they glinted gleefully, she would be up in the air with me in a matter of moments.

I turned dials. I shot downward.

My body bumped into her body as I had intended it to do. My arms closed about her softness, rammed it up against me. I heard her gasp in surprise.

I rather imagine she thought I was panicking, the way a drowning man panics. My clasp about her curving body was nothing more than an instinctive grasp at life itself, in her eyes.

"Take it easy!" she snapped. "You're all right!"

"I'll say I am," I murmured, snuggling closer.

She must have felt my priapic arousal at her loins, the result of her thighs, belly and breasts pressing into me, because she went all red and tried to wriggle free. The more she wriggled, the more she excited me, as she soon found out.

"You're awful," she breathed, her eyes sparking fire. Almost against her will, her hips nudged into me.

The way I figured it, I was taking absolutely no risk at all. From what Beatrice Howard had told me, her boys and girls were living like hermits. She worked them to the bone, she gave them no rest. In her puritanical mind she had figured out that if she kept them too busy to do any more than fall into an exhausted sleep at the end of a working day, she would have no problem with their libidos.

128

So far, she hadn't. But now I was determined to get out from under this crowd of human beings to search that little room behind the door in the Quonset hut lobby. The best way to do this was to get them hung up on the sex life they had been missing out on.

My arms were wrapped about the redhead. Unseen by her, I touched the twin controls of my two belt buckles. I started going down, with my hands fastened in her body stocking. Naturally, the body stocking tore at her shoulders and began sliding down her slimly curved body.

The redhead yelped and put her hands on her gravity belt that was buckled about her waist. The hell with modesty at a time like this! she was thinking. Without the belt, she would fall. So while she held the belt, I held her skintight garment, and drew the damn thing down off her body like an aerial strip tease.

Down below, they thought I was a clumsy oaf.

Somebody yelled, "Go up and give her a hand!"

A dozen voices shouted happily. Up came the girls, closely followed by the lab men. By this time, the body stocking was around her hips. The redhead was bending forward, hissing down at me to stop being so clumsy.

I eyeballed her dangling white breasts and red nipples that were shaking and jouncing to my movements. Seeing how lovely her upper structure was only made me more determined to see what the rest of her was like. I used both hands to grab the thin blue rayon and tug it down past her hips, along her somewhat plump white thighs, to her knees.

Now I could see the shaven mound of her privacy. That she could not cover, since both her hands were too busy holding onto her gravity belt. She was goggling down at me with her big blue eyes, and her breasts were still doing their fleshy dance while her body sought to fight me.

"What are you doing?" she gasped. "You idiot, you're taking my clothes off! Let go, you've got me stark naked!"

"Yeah," I breathed. "Sorry about that, honey."

I yanked the rest of the body stocking loose and let it fall slowly groundward. Now I turned my controls and lifted upward, kissing her left thigh all the way up to her

129

hip. My tongue came out to lave her skin.

She moaned, quivering. Like her boss, Doctor Howard, she had been a long time without loving. I opened my mouth, I fastened soft moist lips on her femininity.

We hung suspended in the air while I made oral love to her. She gasped and shook and went all gooey on me. Her pallid hips bucked wildly to my caresses.

The others could see what was going on as they ascended. They were oddly silent, only the burning eyes in their upturned faces betraying the realization that they too could go a little of this sort of thing.

My redhead was tightening her belt about her naked middle so that the soft flesh bulged above and below the leather. Then her hands slid down to my head, pressing it deeper to her as her thighs widened slowly. At the same time she threw herself backwards so that we began to rotate slowly, forming an aerial acrobatic act of acts.

I was removing my own clothes, sliding down my slacks and shorts, tossing my shirt to the winds, so to speak. My right arm slid upward to clasp her belt and use it as a lever to pull myself upward.

Now I dared to risk a glance about me.

The huge Quonset hut was filled with boys and girls happily stripping one another of their garments. I had set them a fine example, making them realize what they had been missing all these long months they had been working so hard for Doctor Howard.

The air space below their slowly gyrating bodies was filling with body stockings and jockey shorts, lab smocks and trousers dropping groundward until it looked like a surrealistic wash day, without clothes lines. A beefy blonde girl was yelping as she reached across to a male technician who was floating past her. Her fingers grabbed him by his handle and drew him toward her.

Two brunettes were sandwiching a grinning man between their nude bodies, squirming happily on his nudity, fore and aft. An angelic blonde had wrapped her bare legs about the hips of a baby-faced young scientist and was busily engaged in pumping pleasure into both their bodies.

I stabbed upward and into my redhead. She moaned

130

and lay back, floating in the air as though in free-fall. We could not drop, the belts held us suspended in the air and lazily turning over and over as our bodies writhed and twisted where they were joined. It was weird and wild, it was a tri-dimensional turn-on, it was way-out and way-up living graphics.

All about us, other male and female bodies were united and slowly revolving, so that one moment the man was on top, then he was on the bottom, then both man and women were on their sides, lazily drifting. One couple had even assumed the soixante-neuf posture, with her calves hanging past his shoulders, her long blonde hair streaming down between his thighs.

Below me, I heard someone yell.

I peered past the redhead's pale, freckled shoulder down at Beatrice Howard, who was struggling in the arms of the overheated guard. She was trying to battle him, her sweater was half off and hanging by a couple of woolen threads from a bared arm. Her brassiere was jumping around as if trying to throw her breasts out into the open. With her left hand she was trying to slap the guard, since her right hand was too busy hanging onto the skirt he was fighting to pull down.

Her plight suggested that Bea was a little out of her depth in this levitation love-in. She certainly seemed to be refusing the attentions of the guard. But my plan called for the guard to be busy, too, in this aerial aphrodisia.

My companion was too interested in her internal convulsions to notice when I turned down her belt buckle and my twin controls. Our bodies sank slowly through the air, until the action was all over our heads except for the struggle going on between Bea and the guard.

The man with the leathery face and pale blue eyes had stripped himself naked by this time, and was still trying to do the same thing to Doctor Howard. She was having none of it, she was fighting hard and doing a better job of it than she had against me two days before.

I caught the guard with one hand, pushed him toward the redhead who was drifting in the air on her back maybe four feet above the ground, a beatific smile on her mouth.

131

I unfastened my two belts, buckled them around him and shoved him toward the redhead.

He caught on fast. His hand whirled the controls; seconds later, he and the girl were spiraling slowly as they went upward into the air.

Beatrice Howard was sobbing, "Th-this is a-all your f-fault! I've never had any trouble with them and now. . . ."

I said nothing, I just reached for a belt and strapped it about her waist. I grabbed two more for myself. She interrupted me only long enough to gasp, "What do you think you're doing?"

"They need relaxation, honey," I told her. "This is the best thing that could have happened to our organization. You needed loving—you know you did, you admitted it the other day when we were in bed together—so what makes you think these kids are any different from us?"

I was turning her dials, she was lifting upwards into the air. I came after her, just below her high-heeled shoes, getting a look up under her skirts, along her stockinged legs and bare thighs where her garterclasps winked at me.

I reached up my hands, slid them from her ankles upward as my body rose beneath her. My palms did not have to move, my body did the rising, my twin belts lifting me faster than her single belt lifted her. Over warm thigh-flesh beneath nylon stockings, over her bare thighs to her pantied hips, my hands traveled slowly.

Beatrice Howard was staring upward at a couple who were performing the somewhat complicated bamboo cleft position, in which the right foot of the female rests on the left shoulder of the male, while her left leg is stretched out horizontally, tight against his right leg. Bea was licking her lips, studying the to and fro play of female hips and male loins.

Her skirt rose upwards on my forearms as I shoved it out of the way. Her stockinged legs and bare thighs were revealed to the world of the Quonset hut, but everyone else was too busy to pay them any attention. I grabbed her panties, ripped them loose.

"Yes," she whispered suddenly, turning her head so she

132

could stare into my face. "Yes, yes. Do me! Do me! I have a fire inside me, Rod. A fire!"

She lifted her legs. The movement rolled her over in the air until she was on her back. I slipped into position between her thighs. She gave a cry as she felt my priapic splendor entering into her. Her arms came up around me, her heels pressed on the back of my thighs.

Her hips lifted and rotated. Ecstasy gurgled inside her.

"Strip me," she breathed. "Strip me naked while you're doing me. Let them see what I've become through love for you."

My hands went around behind her back as my loins stabbed and jarred her where she lived. My fingers fastened on the snaps of her black brassiere. I undid them, I drew the brassiere straps down her arms and threw the twin-cupped garment and her torn sweater toward the floor.

We were rotating slowly in the air. She grew aware that her heavy breasts were slipping and sliding around on her chest as her body turned over and over. This added to her sensual delight, for I had already discovered that her breasts were extremely sensitive.

My hands caught her breasts, held them while they hung floorward, squeezed them as they lay flat on her chest when she turned around onto her back. I pinched her nipples, I swung them back and forth. She throbbed and pulsed around me, she wailed in her throat and jerked her hips frantically.

My reason told me I must exhaust this woman if I was to have the opportunity to search for some clue as to where to find the Space Travel Limited laboratory. So I concentrated on causing a sexual exhaustion in this woman scientist, of the sort known to the French as *avoir du mal*, a satiation of the senses which produces complete unconsciousness.

It took me half an hour.

When she lay limp in my arms, I dialed us downward. The rest of the levitation love-in was proceeding with all flags flying. The boys and girls were changing partners up there where the painted clouds never moved, devoting themselves to making up for the celibate lives they had been leading.

I placed the comatose Doctor Howard on the floor.

Then I ran for the Quonset hut lobby. The closed door seemed to beckon me. I raced for it. My hand turned the knob, the door was not locked. I walked into a bathroom.

The old ticker sank like a stone falling through air.

All my trouble was for nothing!

But—wait. Hold on, now. There was a door off to one side of the toilet. Maybe that was what I wanted. True, it might be a closet to contain pails and mops for a cleaning lady, but then again—

I opened the door and sagged against the door jamb. I was looking in at two green metal filing cabinets, a small desk with a chair behind it. There was a lounge chair to one side of the desk and beyond the file cabinets was a clothes tree on which were hung a number of garments. Bull's-eye!

I leaped for the desk. It was locked. So were the filing cabinets. I was stark naked, I had no file or bit of celluloid to open the locks. Then it dawned on me. It was just possible that one of the smocks hanging on the clothes tree had a key in its pockets. I found it.

The desk drawers opened and I ransacked them. Nothing! A few letters, none of which told me anything except that Beatrice Howard did not pay her bills on time. I saw a map, neatly folded over. I drew it out and glanced at it.

It was a map of the Exuma Cay section of the Bahama Islands. Nothing there to hold my interest, I'd seen a dozen of them. I put the map down on top of the desk and resumed my search. Five minutes later, as I was replacing the letters and other papers in the drawers, I reached for the map. When I touched it, the paper was warm from the rays of the Bahaman sunlight falling on it through the only window in the room.

I glanced at the map, found my attention caught by a circled dot close by one of the small islands in the chain that runs from Sail Rocks to Hog Cay for almost two hun-

134

dred miles. The dot and circle had not been there before, when I had looked at the map. Of this I was positive.

Secret writing? With lemon juice, that appears when the paper is warmed? Sunlight falling on the map had heated it.

I studied the dot and circle for several seconds. They had been placed to designate an unnamed island not far from Gabber Cay where the Quonset hut stood. I committed the location to memory, then folded the map and—

The door opened. Laura Ogden stood there, staring at me. Just behind her was Beatrice Howard, whose face seemed carved from red clay in her rage. There was a small automatic in Laura Ogden's hand.

"Well," she smiled coldly. "Well, well, well!"

Clever dialogue. I smiled weakly, shaking my head. "Something tells me it isn't so well, Laura."

"You bastard!" screeched Doctor Howard.

She pushed Laura aside and came for me with fingers spread wide, her red fingernails like talons, arms out in front of her nearly naked body. All she wore was a lab smock, which she had no doubt donned hastily. The smock flapped open to her running, revealing that she wore nothing under it.

I fended her off, grabbed her wrists and turned her toward Laura and her automatic. I grinned at Laura over the shoulder of the panting woman who fought me with the fury of a trapped tigress. Her bare heels butted my legs, she turned her face to try and bury her teeth in my hand.

"Better not shoot," I told Laura. "You'll kill the boss."

I felt Beatrice Howard sag against me. "Do-don't shoot," she quavered. "Let him go, Laura."

Laura glanced sharply at the lady boss, then shrugged. "Okay, if you say so. But I wouldn't trust that man if he swore an oath on a mile of Bibles."

"I just want out," I told her. "Go get my slacks and sweater, hon."

Laura turned on a heel and went out through the doorway. I said to Doctor Howard, "You're being smart. You won't get hurt if you behave yourself."

135

I relaxed my muscles. The woman was not fighting me, she appeared to have surrendered. Nor did she make any effort to stop me as I came around the side of the desk and, pushing her ahead of me, walked into the bathroom. This was my mistake.

Two men, hiding on either side of the door, jumped me. Beatrice Howard pulled free, shrieking, "Take him alive, take him alive!"

I felt as if I were already dead, because one of the men bounced a revolver barrel off my skull just as the other rammed a fist into my kidneys. I sagged as my whole body went limp. I started to fall forward.

Bea came to meet me, lifting a bent leg up from her standing pose before me, bashing her dimpled knee into my face. I had a glimpse of her tanned thigh, her black pubic hair and the lower half of her mounded belly a second before the knee hit. After that, except for the one brief spasm of pain that ran through my flesh on the impact, I didn't know a damn thing.

I came to, dripping water.

Beatrice Howard was standing over my naked body. I was trussed up like a fowl for the cooking, with ropes about my wrists and ankles. There was an empty pail of water in her hands. The water that had been inside the pail was splashed all over me.

My head shook weakly. My face felt crushed in.

Laura Ogden was standing beside the doctor, also glaring down at me. She snarled, "Let's cut his pecker off!" Nice girl, Laura.

"No," I managed to get out.

Beatrice Howard smiled cruelly. "I'd thought of that. I've also thought of wiring him to a big spit and cooking him over a fire for a couple of days. But I have a better plan. We'll kill him in such a way that nobody will ever know what happened to him."

The two men who had attacked me were standing behind me. At Bea's orders, they reached down and yanked me to my feet. Walking on either side of my limp body, they dragged me out of the bathroom and into the little lobby of the Quonset hut.

136

They dropped me with a thud on the bare dirt.

I was aware that the boys and girls who had been enjoying the levitation love-in were getting into their clothes. From their silence, I gathered that they were a pretty subdued bunch. The sudden entry of Laura Ogden had made them see themselves as they had been, I imagine, animals up there in the air, rotating and writhing in their passions.

One by one, they filed past my naked body, some of them glancing down at me in mute sympathy. A few averted their eyes; maybe they blamed me for the postcoital malaise they were feeling at the moment. I couldn't have cared less. I had my own private sorrows to put wrinkles in my forehead. To tell the truth, I was scared witless.

The first plans were to castrate me, to cook me over a fire. But these were no good, according to Doctor Howard. What could be worse than that? I lay there in a puddle of my own nervous sweat and shook like a leaf in a sudden gale.

CHAPTER NINE

I woke to the feel of cold steel against my ankles. Somebody had a knife and was slicing into the ropes around my feet, cutting me free. For a brief moment, I thought one of my fellow Coxe Foundation agents had found me. The hope died damn fast when I heard Beatrice Howard talking.

"Don't cut him, I don't want any marks on him." Her voice was hard, cold. She added, "It isn't that I don't want him hurt—I'd love to torture him for a whole year, after the way he played on my womanhood with his masculinity!—but I don't want so much as a single drop of blood spilled, so nobody can tie his death in with Space Travel Limited."

"They'll find my body," I managed to snarl.

Her laughter rang out. "Oh, no they won't. Not ever!"

Callused hands jerked me to my feet. A big man with a florid face and a heavily veined nose from too much elbow-bending at the local bars, tossed me my sports shirt and the slacks I had worn yesterday. I got dressed.

The man poked a gun in my back. "Walk!" he growled.

Beatrice Howard had been standing in front of me, hands on her hips, smartly clad in an art nouveau print dress, belted tightly at her middle. She looked as if she were on her way to a cocktail party. She moved back and away from me as I did what the man said, and walked.

I went out into bright sunlight where I found half a dozen more men, all with revolvers in holsters on their hips, all eyeing me the way a cat does a helpless mouse. I gathered these were the guards who made sure nobody got

138

in or out of places where they were not wanted by Space Travel Limited. The man who had served that purpose yesterday and who had tried to rape Doctor Howard was nowhere around. I wondered, as I stumbled forward, if these guards had done away with him.

The guards walked with me to a high mound covered with wild grasses. I looked up at the sky, dotted here and there with an errant cloud, but for the most part pale blue and flecked with sunshine. It was too nice a day to die.

Doctor Howard gestured. One of the guards opened a small handbag he had been holding and brought out two gravity belts. He strapped them about my middle. My wrists were still tied behind my back. Only my legs were free.

I was a little numb at the moment. My thinking parts were off on strike somewhere. I asked stupidly, "What are those things for?"

Beatrice Howard smiled cruelly. "You're going to find out very soon, Rod. I'm going to turn the dials on each of those gravity belts so that they will lift you upwards, like a slow rocket bound for the moon."

She drew a deep breath and took two steps forward. Her right hand went to the topmost belt that was strapped about my chest. She touched the dial, ran her fingertips over it caressingly, and turned it.

I felt the power surging through the belt, but I did not rise upward. It needed the lifting properties of a second belt for that. Bea ran her palm over the dial controls in the buckle of the second belt, but she did not turn on its power.

Bea said, "You can reflect on your sins all the way to outer space, Rod. Once you get up into the atmosphere, you'll find it very cold. I just hope you don't freeze to death before you have a chance to think back on your failure. I want your death slow and painful in coming. I think it will. You aren't going to die all at once. You're going to have time to think and think while you wait for death to come and find you."

Maybe she wanted me to beg. I knew I would get no mercy from her, her hard face and cold eyes told me that

139

much, so I would not give her the satisfaction. I stared up at the pale blue Bahaman sky and fluffy white clouds in the distance, and I tried to appear as nonchalant as possible even though I was damn near dying of fright inside me.

"Nice day for a trip," I managed to get out.

Beatrice Howard stepped forward two paces and let me have the flat of her hand across my cheek. "Bastard! Double-crossing bastard!"

I looked at her and made my lips smile. "You can kill me, honey—but something tells me I've won our personal little war."

She screeched and leaped for me. Laura Ogden and a couple of big guards jumped for her. They grabbed her and while she wriggled furiously, Laura panted, "No, Doctor Howard, no! You don't want him to come down with scratch marks on his cheeks if anything should go wrong with the belts!"

Beatrice Howard shook her body, nodding so that her black hair came tumbling down across one side of her face. "Y-yes, Laura. You're ri-right."

She pushed back from the men, her hands going to her hair, rearranging and straightening it. Her face was a rigid white mask out of which her eyes burned like black diamonds. There was no pity, no mercy, in her face; it was like the face of a conqueror who sees his foes before him for the killing.

"I know you don't pray, so I won't ask you to," she snapped, and came to stand before me. Her fingers caught the dials of the second control belt and whipped them to full power.

I shot skyward like a bullet.

My eyes were closed in that first rush of speed, but I opened them to stare down at the upturned faces below me. Doctor Howard and Laura Ogden were smiling, the burly men were expressionless. I thought they all should be a little more excited. As far as I knew, they were looking at history. Nobody had ever been executed this way before.

Then my bravado fell away.

140

"No!" I screamed. "I don't want to die!"

I am afraid I cursed the Coxe Foundation and Walrus-moustache up and down and sideways while I was lifting up into the air. Until this moment, I doubted very much whether Beatrice Howard had ever used her gravity belts out of doors in the daytime. I hoped against hope somebody would see me, maybe somebody cruising the Exuma Cays in a speedboat.

Then I thought, "What good will that do me?"

By the time anyone could flash an alarm I would be up to the topmost limits of the exosphere bordering on the rim of space. I would be heading for the moon and damn near frozen to death if I weren't already dead from the lack of oxygen.

Beneath me the land spread away to the green cays, the water like a field of sparking diamonds in the sunlight. I made out a couple of yachts, and a number of cabin cruisers, far away. They were slightly larger than big dots, this high up. I doubted if they could have seen me if they'd been looking right at my rising body.

It was getting harder to breathe.

My teeth were chattering from the cold.

My mind was getting numb too, because it seemed to be throbbing and roaring deep inside my skull. I listened to the sound my mind made. Did all dying people experience this sensation? The sound was getting louder.

I struggled with the ropes that held my wrists behind me, I flailed with my legs, but none of it did any good. I went on rising and the sound got louder and louder.

"Rod! Rod Damon!"

Now I was hearing voices! Maybe there was a heaven, after all, and the angels were coming to get me. I am not ashamed to say there were tears in my eyes. I drew several deep gulps of air.

I gasped, "I'm re-ready—I—I guess."

Something touched my head and fell away. An angel was reaching for me! I babbled hysterically, laughing and crying. There was nothing up here but me and the clouds. Even the birds were far below me, by this time.

Again I felt that brush of angel fingers.

141

"Rod! Rod!"

It was the voice of an angel, all right. A female angel. It was vaguely familiar too. At the time, I must have been more than somewhat out of my skull, because I began to think about the women I have known, and none of them was a candidate for angelhood. Now the sound in my head was ear-splitting.

I saw a helicopter and a girl in cowboy clothes with a ten-gallon hat on her head and a lasso in her hand. She was leaning out of the open door of the chopper craft, reeling out the lasso while the whirlybird was rising upward just above me.

"Angel," I breathed. "I do know you!"

It was Wanda Weaver Yule. Now I could make out the bulk of Walrus-moustache huddled in the space behind Wanda and the chopper driver.

"I love you both," I moaned happily.

If I had been in any doubt before, I knew I was nuts now, telling the Chief that I loved him. Tears were streaming down my cheeks, there was a silly grin on my lips. I watched that lariat come for me the way a drowning man sees a life preserver twirling through the air.

The lasso looped around me, pinning my arms against my sides. The loop tightened and I felt the sudden drag of the helicopter.

Wanda was laughing and crying as her hands caught my belt and yanked me in. I fell across her lap, face up. She put her arms around me and began kissing me all over my cold, tear-wet face.

"Baby—baby—what've they done to you?" she babbled.

The Chief was more prosaic. He got out a pocket-knife and sawed away at the ropes binding my wrists until my hands were free. They were so numb, my arms were so stiff that Wanda had to reach behind me and draw my hands out from behind my back, one after the other.

She chafed my hands between her palms to restore my circulation. She whispered, "Poor darling, they're like ice. Here." She put my hands under her hot little armpits and tightened her arms on them. The heat felt real good. So

142

did Wanda Weaver Yule, who was all over perfume and soft flesh. I nested my head against her shoulder.

Walrus-moustache always has to spoil a tender moment. "What are those things you're wearing? They the gravity belts we've talked about?"

I nodded, muttering, "One belt will lift a hundred and fifty pounds. They needed two for me."

"I'll take them," he snapped, and yanked them off.

He was too busy studying the belts to pay me any attention, so I put my lips into the soft vee of Wanda's red satin cowgirl shirt and kissed her in the vale of her breasts. She gurgled contentment, cuddling me.

"Imagine destroying you," she crooned. "What a waste for the women of the world!"

"Yeah," I breathed, nodding happily.

It was taking me some little time to realize that I would not die, that I was still alive. I had been so near death, there had seemed so little hope—so little? there had been no hope at all!—that I still was not myself.

"What are you doing here?" I asked her big breasts.

She giggled, "You remember I told you how I was considering a return to the rodeo circuit? But what I needed was a new act, something with sock? Well, thanks to your marvelous boss-man, I came up with something.

"Rod, I'm going to fly down over a rodeo—say, at some open place like Pendleton or Cheyenne—rope a calf and fall on it from a choppercraft instead of from a horse. Don't you think that'll be sensational?"

"Right, honey—almost as sensational as you are!"

I fell asleep talking to her bosom.

They woke me up as the helicopter landed on Grand Bahama island. I could walk, but the pilot was close beside me until I got into the little car the Chief had rented, along with the seaside villa where Midge Priest and Wanda Weaver Yule were his guests.

A doctor filled me full of drugs so that I slept for about twenty hours in a queen-size bed with four mahogany posters and a ruffled chintz valance. It was a female-type room, with chintz drapery on the chairs, the vanity bench and the small night tables that flanked the bed.

143

I lay there awhile, staring at the top of the bed, thanking my lucky stars for the fact that I was warm, alive, and damn hungry, rather than soaring outward into space behind the exosphere. I could eat, I could make love. I could breathe in fragrant air and bask once more in warm tropical sunlight.

"Yaaa-hoooh!" I bellowed.

I leaped out of bed and opened the closet door. I am familiar enough by this time to know how old Walrus-moustache works. He growls, he breathes dragon-fire, he rants and bellows, but he treats his agents like crown princes, at the very least. Nothing is too good for them, so long as they do their jobs.

My clothes hung in the closet, my shoes were on the floor. A new shoulder-holster, straps dangling, hung on a closet peg, with a Colt .45 automatic thrusting from the brown leather sheath. Quite happily, I grabbed slacks and a sweater, and carrying the shoulder holster and the Colt downstairs, I moved in on the breakfast table.

I dined in solitary, since it was close to ten in the morning. The maid told me everybody else was out on the beach, getting some sun. So after my ham and eggs, scrambled, plus a pot of coffee and some crumbcake, I sauntered out onto the white sands and stood admiring Midge Priest in a black bikini and Wanda Weaver Yule in a white bikini that set off her sun-bronzed skin to perfection. Even the Chief, in his droopy swim trunks, looked good to my happy eyes.

Midge yelped and ran to me. I caught her, kissed her for several seconds, until Wanda yanked her away and kissed me herself. I put both arms about their bare middles and walked to the grinning man sitting on the beach blanket and holding up his hand for me to shake. Old Walrus-moustache actually looked human, for a change.

"I know this isn't the time to bring up business," he began, when I interrupted him.

"Oh, but it is. I want to get back there and pay off that Howard crowd for what they did to me."

"Smashing their Quonset hut isn't going to do us much good," the boss-man pointed out. "We have to hit them in

144

their heartland, at their laboratory."

"I think I know where it is," I gloated.

I told him about the circle and dot on the map I had found, that had revealed itself when the hot Bahaman sunlight had touched it. "If that doesn't mark where their lab is, I'm a cockeyed wombat. It's got to be there. I'm going to find out if it is."

"We'll all go," said Wanda, beaming up at me. "My yacht is in Freeport harbor, ready to weigh anchor. We'll go on a sightseeing cruise across the Exumas. When we come to where that circle and dot is, you can drop overside and go for your swim."

We lounged in the sun for another hour.

Then we all piled into the big yacht Wanda Weaver Yule owned, and set out across Northwest Providence Channel, moving past the Great Stirrup lighthouse by noon. Walrus-moustache stationed himself in the yacht's radio room, where he was busy alerting the fighting forces of the Coxe Foundation to be ready when and if we needed them. I was in the gear room, selecting fins, undersea goggles and other assorted diving equipment.

Midge was busy helping me.

Well, maybe not exactly helping me. She was undoing my shirt and slacks, getting them off so I could don a pair of swimtrunks. She was still in her micro-bikini that exposed all but a few vital areas of her female body to the elements and men's eyes. I was discovering, glancing from the way her breasts sagged heavily into her nylon bikini cups and the manner in which the thin straps of her micro-trunks dented her soft hipflesh, that I was fully alive again.

Erotologists say men are more excited by a partially hidden female body than they are by an entirely naked one. This is because there is mystery involved; the male does not see the hidden charms of the female he looks at, and so his imagination and the subconscious 'mate image' which he possesses, born of prior experiences that date all the way back to childhood, are necessarily involved. The hidden parts, bolstered by mystery and imagination, become even more pleasing; the desire to strip the clothing

145

off and see the unadorned female is part and parcel of his aroused sex interest. Conditioned to act according to the mores of his time and society, the male cannot do this, so the desire to do so enhances his sexual attraction toward the clothed or partially clothed female.

Anyhow, I was reacting to this almost-complete exposure of female flesh, and Midge Priest was glad I was. She cooed and oohed at sight of my return to good health, patting and stroking me with ardent appraisal.

"Do you think we could?" she breathed, eyes glistening.

"We could, but we won't," I told her.

When she pouted, I leaned forward to kiss her lips. "I have a job to do, honey. I'll need all my energy, like a soldier going into battle. In the old days, men who went out to fight were forbidden to carnally know a woman, as the historians so graciously put it. Go read your history from its original sources if you don't believe me."

"Oh, I believe you," Midge nodded. "It's just that it seems such a shame. You're right there, I'm right here, and we mustn't do anything about it."

"I'll be back before nightfall," I promised.

The *Yuletide* was making twelve knots across Exuma Sound. The island marked with a circle and dot was off our starboard side. Walrus-moustache was standing at the rail, studying the little cay with powerful field-glasses. As I approached he took them away from his eyes and turned to me.

"I don't see a thing. Are you sure this is the spot?" he groused.

"I'm sure. Here, let me take those things."

I looked, but all I saw were coral growths, a little reef, a high cliff behind which the tiny island showed like the humped back of a dead monster drowned in water. Trees covered most of the island, except where the sand ran down out of the forest to merge with the frothing waters of Exuma Sound. The island was empty of all life.

I shook my head, lowering the glasses. "It's got to be this one, or I've been wasting my time down here. Let me go scuba diving, chief. Maybe I can find something."

146

I went down over the port side, so anyone watching the yacht from the cay would see nothing. I swam down under the yacht, and set out for the islet. I swam easily, the water was warm, and I made good time.

Up ahead of me I could see the beach sloping upward, the white sands gleaming in the shallow, clear waters. To my left, the dark rock formation of the high cliff stabbed downward. I was turning to move toward the beach, intending to step onto the island and search it for the laboratory, when my attention was caught by a moray eel that came into view slowly.

I saw its head first, as if thrust out of solid rock, then the rest of its five-foot body as it slid upward and, at sight of me, darted off into the shoals. Apparently it had emerged from a hole in the rock cliff.

I veered left and swam forward, fins kicking. As I came closer, I saw the water glow brightly as if to hidden lights. My hands went out, gripped a thin wall of coral. I drew myself forward, peered over the other side.

Perhaps five feet down the water was very bright. I saw the true wall of the cliff, broken off to show a big rectangle of light. The coral wall to which I clung was like a screen, hiding that opening from any observer. I inched over the wall, diving down.

I swam through the growing lightness in the waters, under the true cliffwall, and beneath a ten-foot span of that cliff. I knew I was approaching an undersea cavern and my heart was slamming excitedly. Could this be the hidden laboratory that nobody seemed able to find? There was no more perfect hiding place, for if I was right in my conjectures, it was invisible to the outer world. The only way you could get at it was to swim through this submarine tunnel.

The water was like white fire all about me. I dared not rise to the surface because if this was a cavern that held a laboratory, I would be spotted—and no doubt shot down without hesitation.

I glided along one of the undersea cave walls, clinging to little projections and encrustations to make sure I

147

would not bob to the surface. I searched along the cavern wall until I found a background of dark stone forming the wall section at this point.

Very gradually, hoping my hair would blend in against the dark stone behind me, I lifted my head above water, removing my goggles.

I guess I gawked a few seconds in stunned amazement. There was a laboratory here, all right, built into the rock walls of the cavern. Men and women were moving about in their lab smocks—I recognized a number of them from the levitation love-in—busy at their tasks. The cave itself was a couple hundred feet high and eight hundred or more feet deep. It was brilliantly lighted, which accounted for the brightness of the waters in this hidden cavern pool. The hum of machinery explained how the cavern was fed with fresh air from the outside which was periodically filtered, cleaned, and fed back into the cavern.

I took a long, slow look around so I might describe the place to Walrus-moustache. It should not be hard to pull a surprise attack on the installation, there were a couple of guards lounging off to one side, but nobody was looking at the pool or at my head poking from the water.

I submerged slowly, so that hardly a ripple could be seen. I did not begin my swim until I was a few feet above the bottom of the pool. Then I made all speed possible toward the cave entrance.

Half an hour later I was sitting, dripping wet, on the deck of the *Yuletide,* making my report. "There must be another way out of the cave, maybe through a tunnel on the landward side, because I doubt very much if Doctor Howard would let her lab technicians come swarming up out of the water. They'd be visible to any chance passerby who might get curious about a swarm of boys and girls appearing so miraculously off the coast of a supposedly uninhabited island like this."

The Chief nodded. "I'll notify our attack units to go on the alert. They ought to be here in a little while, it's only an hour or two by air from the Florida coast. We could even attack by midnight, except that we wouldn't catch anybody in the lab that late."

So, the next day was set as the attack time. Until then, I was more or less on my own, I thought. Not so you could notice it. I had to talk to a Foundation artist whom the Chief had flown from the mainland to the Yule yacht, so he could draw pictures of the lab, to give the attackers an idea of what they could expect to find waiting for them.

When I was through talking and he was through drawing, we had a pretty good picture of what I had seen in those few moments I had been staring at the cave laboratory. It was almost nine o'clock at night, by this time.

Midge had been hanging around me ever since dinnertime, until the boss-man shooed her off to bed. She had been wearing a see-through dress with just her own sweet self under it. Teasingly tantalizing. She saw that she was getting to me, and as if to give me a shot of extra sock, she posed in light that turned her see-through gown to absolute mist.

However, old Walrus-moustache brought me a doctor instead of Midge when the artist was finished. "Stick a needle in him," the Chief growled. "He has to get a good night's sleep."

So I got a needle instead of Midge to take to bed.

Honesty being one of my virtues, I must admit I almost slept around the clock. The Chief woke me at eight the next morning with a cheery order to get up, get armed, and get cracking.

The Coxe Foundation was going on the attack.

We were to hit the laboratory about three in the afternoon. Fifty expert swimmers and expert marksmen were already on deck, fully armed, ready to form the attack detail. There were sea-sleds fitted with machine guns in waterproof mountings; each man was armed with a revolver, also in a waterproof sheathing, and a long knife. Two teams of four men each were assigned to the twin sea-sleds.

Our little army was lowered over the port side of the yacht, just as I had let myself down the day before. One by one, with a kick of black rubber fins, while some of the men pushed the sea-sleds ahead of them, we went down into the greenish-blue depths beneath the *Yuletide.*

It was my job to act as guide.

I brought the little army to the edge of the coral wall where I had seen the moray eel. My hand signaled them that I was going to dive. The sea-sled boys must be careful in the rock tunnel. They must not let their yellow-painted sea-sleds scrape against the tunnel walls so as to give the alarm.

I swam through the brightly lighted waters, stroking forward toward the low shelf of the cave floor. When I came up out of the water, the sea-clad soldiers were to open up with the machine guns.

I counted up two hundred, then started crawling up the stone shelf leading to the laboratory. The guards were to my right. The sea-sled machine guns would be firing in that direction. At the number two hundred one, I stepped up onto the coral shelf, stripping off the sheathing for my automatic.

The lab workers were all busy, bent above the glass retorts and test tubes, testing machines and gravity chambers. None of them saw me. Only the guards came out of their lazy stances, reaching for their weapons.

I turned my head. Not a single head, not one sea-sled, had come up dripping from the water. I was alone—a perfect target for the guns turning in my direction—as I tried hastily to bring my finned feet up onto the laboratory floor.

I snapped off a shot at the guards.

I missed.

The guards—there were eight of them—would not miss. I found myself looking down the muzzles of eight automatic assault rifles, with eight hard faces nuzzled into their stocks, with eight fingers curled about their triggers. All hell erupted then.

I flung myself facedown onto the lab floor. The eight rifles spat a hail of hot lead right where I had been standing.

At the same time I heard the spatter of a machine gun raining a leaden curtain into the cavern. It was joined a moment later by the chatter of its mate. The eight guards were pinned to the rock wall behind them, dead on their

150

feet. Blood ran in a line across their chests where the machine-gunners had laid their patterns.

I got up and ran. I snapped a shot at a rack of test-tubes where two girl technicians were standing, big of eye and with their lipsticked mouths wide open. The glass shattered all over them. The girls screamed and fell.

Up ahead of me I could see Doctor Howard, rising to her feet from behind a laboratory counter where she had been conducting an experiment. I paused only to kick off my rubber fins; running in those things was damn difficult. My pause gave her the opportunity she wanted.

She turned and reached with both hands toward a segment of the rock wall that was inlaid with a metal control board containing levers in its slots. I did not know what those levers would do, but instinct told me it would not be nice.

I raised my gun, my finger squeezed trigger.

The bullet hit the control panel inches from Beatrice Howard. She flinched back; she would not have been human if she had not; but then, with a repressed cry of sheer hatred and despair, she lunged again.

This time, I was close enough to reach out.

I caught her, whirled her around. For an instant I thought she was going to collapse in sheer horror as she turned her eyes to my face for the first time. In the goggles and with the aqualung harness on my chest and back, I was more or less in disguise. But up this close, she got a good look at me.

"Aieeee!" she screamed.

Her face went white and her shapely legs threatened to buckle under her. She put out her hands as if to feel my solidity. She breathed, "You—you're alive! But you can't be! No power on Earth could have saved you."

I laughed down at her. The two of us were ignoring the rest of the maelstrom that was the cave laboratory exploding around our ears in a cacophony of bullets and shattering glass and metal. A man bumped me; a girl was screeching less than three yards away in unholy terror.

"Wanda Weaver Yule saved me—in a helicopter."

Her eyes got enormous. She ran her eyes back and forth

on my face, as if to see whether I was mocking her. Then she whirled and dove once more for the levers.

My left hand shot out, caught her by the front of her lab smock and sent her flying backwards. She stumbled, her feet slipping on the spilled chemicals and broken glass lining the lab floor. I wanted to run to her, to catch her. She was falling straight for a big iron block that was used as a testing device. It had about a dozen gravity belts strapped around it.

She thudded into the iron block.

To my intense surprise, instead of returning to the attack, Beatrice Howard clawed her way to the top of the block. Her hand reached down, began turning the buckle-dials of the belts. The iron block, with Doctor Howard crouching on top of it, started to rise.

I yelled, and leaped.

The block was a good four feet above the cavern floor. I had to jump in order to get a hand on one of the belts. The iron itself was too smooth to afford me a handhold, so my fingers closed down like a vise on a leather belt.

The woman atop the block looked down at me, grinning the way the Gorgon must have grinned at its victims. I was helpless, too busy hanging on for dear life to attack her.

She could attack me, however. Her red fingernails clawed for my face as she leaned out over the edge of the slowly lifting block. The cavern ceiling was so far above its floor that from that height, I would be fit food for a large chunk of blotting paper if I fell.

And I was going to fall. Her long red nails were right at my eyes. It was all I could do to turn my head this way and that to prevent being blinded.

152

CHAPTER TEN

I reached up with my right hand, dangling precariously from a leather belt—hoping it would hold together—and tried to cuff Doctor Howard. She laughed at my futile attempts. She drew back a little onto the iron block so I could not quite reach her.

"You're going to die, Rod," she panted maliciously. "They're going to have to scrape what's left of you off the lab floor with a knife."

I put my right hand on a belt higher up.

Please hold, I prayed to that belt. Dear God, don't let that buckle loosen! I moved upward about a foot. My body was swaying back and forth and it was tilting the iron block slightly so that Doctor Howard slid sideways a little.

She yelped, fastening her fingers to the edge of the block.

I went up another foot, reaching with my left hand for another belt. I swayed my body more than somewhat, because I could see my swinging weight was making the block tilt even more.

My eyes went upward. There was an opening in the cavern ceiling, and a sort of flat platform there, of polished wood. Behind it, I seemed to see part of a room. I had no time to spend on sight-seeing, however. Beatrice Howard was screeching at me like a maniac, reaching down to run her sharp fingernails across the back of my left hand, trying to make me release my hold. I gritted my teeth against the pain as I saw five red, bloody furrows appear on the back of my left hand. Spots jumped in front of my eyes. I did not dare look below me where the broken

153

glass and shattered metal of the laboratory was waiting to catch me.

My right hand went up. It landed on a cheek.

Doctor Howard screamed. I could feel the block tilting crazily as her body slid across its smooth top. I waited for the sudden drop in the weight on the iron block and the resultant increase in its speed of lift that would tell when her body went over the edge.

Then to my horror, I looked upward.

The block was just a few feet below the opening where the polished wood platform waited. I was below the platform. There was room in the opening for the solid block. When the block lifted into place, the platform would scrape me loose from my precarious hold. I would fall to the floor.

I tried to swallow. My mouth was too dry.

So I climbed. I never moved so fast in my life. My right hand grabbed the topmost belt, my left hand went to hook its fingers on the edge of the block top. I pulled myself upwards.

As my head came above the level of the block top, I saw Beatrice Howard crouched on the opposite side, glaring at me as she clung to her little perch. She did not dare attack, any movement of hers would have pitched her over the side. She could only cling there and hate me with her blazing eyes and writhing lips as I drew myself upward on top of the block.

The iron block slid into place.

It fitted neatly into the opening. My feet were toward the wooden platform, so I backed up on my hands and knees until I was inside a modernistically furnished office, fitted out with deep wall-to-wall carpeting, with a huge desk and swivel chair, with filing cabinets hidden behind a folding screen, hanging bookshelves on the walls, and various plaques, masks and pictures that made this concealed office a neat little pad.

Beatrice Howard was standing on the block now, and advancing toward me. To my surprise, I saw she was smiling. "It was a good fight while it lasted," she said. "I

154

have to hand it to you, Rod—you're quite a man when it comes to a fight or a frolic."

"Yeah," I said drily, waiting for the punch line.

My eyes searched her lush body for a weapon. Her lab smock hung open over a too-tight sweater that showed off her heavy breasts, sagging gently and moving up and down and sideways in that bobbling motion which brassieres were invented to prevent. Her hips firmed outward into a too-tight skirt. No weapon could have existed unnoticed under those garments.

Eyes fastened on mine, she shrugged out of the smock, arms behind her, breasts shaking even more ripely as she hunched her shoulders to let the smock drop down her arm.

"I have a million and a half dollars in good American cash in the office safe, Rod," she said. "Why don't you and I form a team? We could get away from that debacle down below. I have a secret cove not far from here where I keep a speedboat against emergencies."

"No, thanks," I said.

She eyed me closely. "I'll pay you half of that million and a half—to let me get away. Nobody'll ever know."

Her swaying hips were in my line of vision as she moved across the carpeting to a big oil painting. Her red-nailed hand thrust the painting back. There was a safe dial set into the wall. She glanced at me archly over a shoulder.

"Mind if I get the money out?"

"Go ahead. I'll have to turn it over to the Foundation, anyhow."

She turned the dial back and forth.

The safe door came open. Doctor Howard reached inside it. Stupid me! When it comes to a female, I am always a little more trusting than I should be. Her hand went in, but when it came out, instead of good American cash it held a good American Colt revolver.

The revolver pointed at me.

The revolver was being fired.

Something hit my shoulder with the kick of a Missouri

mule. My knees buckled, but they held long enough for me to reach the woman in the too-tight clothes. My right hand slammed at the gun, driving it sideways. My left fist rammed into the side of her jaw.

She reeled backwards, arms flailing as she tried to recover her balance. The Colt blasted again, putting a hole in one of the walls, up near the ceiling. Through a fog caused by the pain in my wound, I staggered after her.

I picked up a standing ashtray and threw it. The metal base took her across the belly, half driving the wind from her lungs. The Colt sent red flame at the carpeted floor. I dived for her.

My shoulder hit her sideways, at her left knee, and sent her flying through the air to land on the polished platform and slide along it. I got a fast look up her legs, along stockinged thighs and bare thighs, right up to the darkness where her panties normally went. She was not wearing panties. I thought again that she had become a changed woman in a lot of ways.

Beatrice Howard screamed.

Her sliding body hit the top of the iron block. It unbalanced it, sent it crashing against the slot-wall that held it. I heard the grate of metal as the belt-buckles rammed the wall.

In some manner, the sudden jar caused about five of the buckle controls to go off. The iron block dropped from its perch beside the polished wooden platform.

Doctor Howard screamed.

I staggered to the edge of the platform, staring downward. Below me I saw the descending block, with Beatrice Howard clinging to it with her hands. Her terrified face was turned up to me. The block was beginning to tilt over, too, without the lifting powers of those five belts.

"Help me!" she screamed. "Rod—I'm going to die if you don't!"

My wounded shoulder was killing me. I had all I could do to stand there on the platform rim without collapsing. I saw her slide off the block, begin her fall. She looked like a straw doll turning over and over, lazily, all the time screaming at the top of her lungs.

156

Her body hit the lab floor and bounced.

The huge iron block settled down on top of her.

I felt sick. I could see her head and a foot stuck out from under the block. I moved backward on the platform and lay flat on my back. My senses were deserting me. I would lie here and wait for somebody to come and get me, I decided.

Of course, I might bleed to death in the meantime. Somehow, I just didn't care. My memory went on telling me how Beatrice Howard had lifted a hand to that block as it came down. She had been alive when that weight had descended slowly on her writhing body.

I was still flat on my back, but now I was in bed.

Midge Priest was standing to one side of the bed, drawing my pajama trousers off my hairy legs. She was being very gentle about it; I hadn't felt a thing until just now, when her tuggings moved my hips.

"Well, hello there," I greeted her.

She turned startled eyes at me. Her forefinger went to her lips, giving me the silence gesture. Midge looked very delectable in a black satin evening gown cut down to where her bellybutton played wink with light and shadow. Her big white breasts bulged out the panels that were supposed to cover them. Her stiff nipples made dots in the black satin.

"I got away as soon as I could," she whispered.

"Good for you," I grinned.

I was lying there stark naked except for a bandage about my shoulder. She was fully dressed. The fact that her eyes were caressing my priapic pride was enough to set me off, I was discovering. I looked past my chest at my rising self. Midge was making funny noises in her throat.

"They're still eating in the dining room," she told me when the gurgling sounds stopped. "You're in the Yule beach villa, in case you don't know. They brought you here last night so the doctors could bandage you up. You've been sleeping for a hell of a long time, in case you don't know that either."

"I do feel rested," I admitted.

157

She was raising the evening gown skirt. "I hope you are, Rod. I really do. Because I'm going to leave here tomorrow morning with your boss to give evidence in the trial about the Yule-lift crowd. And that means I'll be a material witness under guard. I won't be allowed any visitors."

The skirt was up to her knees. She frowned, looking down at me. "You can't see me too well, with me on the floor. Here, let me step up on this chair."

She pulled a chair away from the little writing desk and, yanking her skirts up to her garterclasps, showed me all her stockinged legs as she stepped up. She stood there and went on raising her skirt hem.

"You can see me now, can't you? Oh, my, yes, you can. You're paying me the perfect tribute, Rod darling. Look how big you're getting!"

I guess I was, at that. I didn't want to look away from those two shapely legs to check it. High-heeled shoes, black nylon stockings, bare female thighs, white and plump, a couple of garters—black Lastex and red lace bisecting those thighs—and I was off in a voyeuristic heaven.

Midge panted, "This night has got to last me a long time, Rod. Please darling, say you understand! I know you're wounded and all, but——"

"I'm not wounded there," I pointed out with perfect logic.

"No, you aren't," she nodded, eyes big and wide.

"You'll have to do all the work. All I can do is lie here. Well, maybe that's not all I can do, but as far as moving around, forget it."

"I'm not wounded. I can move—and how I'll move! Here, look at this little surprise, sweetie."

The black satin hem went up to her hips. Under the evening gown she was wearing skimpy black nylon and red lace divided panties. They consisted of two leg openings and a panel across the belly. An empty, inverted vee showed off her intimate parts, full of fluffy blonde hair.

"I like it, I like it," I reiterated.

Her blue eyes were slumbrous. "I thought you might,
158

that's why I bought them. Just for you."

The hem rose to her navel. The divided panties were worn over her garterbelt, they did not detract from her ability to perform any number of love-in positions, but they damn well did add to her attractiveness.

The gown lifted to her armpits. Her breasts were gently swinging globes of blue-veined white flesh. Midge giggled, watching my eyes dance from one dark red nipple to the other, back and forth, as they shook and jiggled in an appeal to my manhood.

"Get ready, Rod," she breathed. "I have to get me enough tonight to make up for all the lonely nights coming up in some hotel room, where I'll be waiting for that trial, all alone behind a locked door."

"Come and get it, honey," I wheedled.

The evening gown went flying across the room, Midge stepped down off the chair and came toward me, bare arms extended to their full length as she went on shimmying for my benefit. She giggled, bending over. Her breasts dangled, brushing their nipples against my *zist,* as the French sometimes name the male organ.

My hips squirmed pleasurably.

"Well, come on," I growled.

Her laughter was wicked, sensual. "Is big mans in such a hurrykins?" she whispered, breasts swaying back and forth, scratching my flesh.

"Damn right I am," I growled, reaching my right hand from her bare back, sliding my palm down the soft flesh to her garterbelt. "Move closer, my little Venus fly-trap—I can't move my left arm without hurting, but I can move my right."

"Uh-uh. I do everything. Remember? I bribed one of the doctors attending you to give me a number of vitamin shots. I'm determined to find out just how much of a hold on you that priapism has. I'm going to bring you down to where us poor mortals live, Rod. Rod! What a name for a guy like you. Wowww!"

Her soft palm slid across my hairy upper thigh. It caressed me gently, quivering as her own libido reacted to the fondlings she bestowed on my maleness. Midge leaned across the bed, putting her left cheek down on my belly.

She began licking me slowly with her wet tongue. Her painted red mouth gaped to caress, to please. I was moaning deep in my throat.

"We don't need the prelims," I panted.

"I want you to last," she breathed.

"It's you I'm worried about," I grated as her teeth closed down. "You'll poop out long before I do."

She crawled onto the bed, resting on her nyloned knees, smiling down at me. "Won't I? Won't I last? I'll show you, mister man."

A stockinged leg lifted, swung over my loins. Midge lowered herself, gripping and fitting me to her need. As she sank into complete ecstasy, she gave a shrill cry.

"All night long?" I challenged.

"All—night—long," she nodded, settling her hips to their task of driving the two of us buggy.

She almost made it, at that.

Five hours and twenty-three orgasms later, Midge Priest sagged limply down on top of me. There was no more strength left in her. She was snoring gently three seconds after she laid her head on my unwounded shoulder.

I was something of a spent spy myself. The things I do for my country! Well, in a manner of speaking, Midge had been my country—where I really lived—for a little while.

Just an old country boy. That's me.

www.ingramcontent.com/pod-product-compliance
Ingram Content Group UK Ltd.
Pitfield, Milton Keynes, MK11 3LW, UK
UKHW022255280225
455674UK00001B/28